BirthRight

La Patron Series – Book One
The Alphas Alpha

Sydney Addae

BirthRight: Book one of the La Patron Series
Sydney Addae
Copyright 2013 by Addae, Sydney
First Edition Electronic April 2013
Published by Sitting Bull Publications, LLC

This is a work of fiction. Names, places, characters, and incidents are either the product of the author's imagination or are used fictitiously, and any resemblance to any actual persons, living or dead, businesses, organizations, events, or locales is entirely coincidental. All trademarks, service marks, registered trademarks, and registered service marks are the property of their respective owners and are used herein for identification purposes only. The publisher does not have any control over or assume any responsibility for the author or third-party websites or their contents.

All rights reserved under the International and Pan-American Copyright Conventions. No part of this book may be reproduced or transmitted in any form or by any means, electronic or mechanical, including photocopying, recording, or by any information storage and retrieval system, without permission in writing from Sydney Addae.

BirthRight

Book One
La Patron, the Alphas Alpha

When you're the top wolf on the continent with the backing of the Goddess, how does an enemy topple your kingdom? By challenging you to a fight? No. By changing the rules.

After three hundred years of fighting and service to the Goddess, Silas Knight is the Patron, Alpha to the Alphas on the North American continent. As the top wolf, he fears little and has seen most things. But when he discovers someone or something has been quietly disturbing the natural order of things, he's surprised. Certain human women can birth fully functioning wolves, and that's a major problem.

Jasmine Bennett has no idea her deceased husband was a wolf shifter or that her twin sons are shifters. Her life changes when she rushes to her son's bedside after he's wounded in Afghanistan and returned stateside. Now her life's in danger because of her ability to give birth to a breed of beings she never knew existed.

Chapter 1

TIGHT-LIPPED, SILAS KNIGHT stepped off the private jet. Security was tight, as it should be. A costly mistake had occurred. Cameron, his godson, should not be in this military facility. Worse, the officers in charge refused to release him to the shifter hospital in the same area.

His anger buffeted everyone within proximity. Alphas, who had come from multiple states, bowed in respect as he strode toward the car that would transport him to the hospital.

"La Patron," the local Alpha, Jayden Knight, murmured, head bowed. "Welcome to Bethesda. A car is prepared to take you to the Hospital where a shifter doctor has taken over the case. Cameron's papers are drawn and his transfer is awaiting your inspection."

"Good, thank you." He turned and gazed at all those who had come in deference to his visit and nodded. "I will be here for a few days. We will meet and discuss matters of importance with you soon. I look forward to talking with you."

The somber faces smiled graciously. Their excitement tangible in the stale air of the hangar. Despite his godson's condition, life went on, and these men had pressing concerns to discuss with him. Keeping his face neutral, he waited until his security detail gave him a nod, and entered the car. Under normal conditions, he would have bought his car. But appearances needed to be maintained.

At least for now.

* * *

"I apologize for the mix-up, your Honor," the doctor said in low tones. "It appears the commander in Afghanistan who normally handles these transfers was in the field. Your godson departed with a few other injured soldiers to Germany instead of France. Later, they shipped him here. The attending physicians did not have a chance to look at him. I took over within an hour of his arrival. The head physician wanted to have a team examine him before approving the transfer to the specialty hospital," the smaller man said as he walked alongside Silas.

At the last comment, Silas stopped and raised his brow.

"None of them did," the doctor rushed to say. "I brought in another team who approved the change of venue."

"I am disappointed over such a break-down in the system. We have people in place all over the world to prevent these incidents. Now, I must decide if this happens often. The military notified me because I am listed as his next of kin. Otherwise, I would have had no knowledge of the fuck-up."

The doctor swallowed hard and followed Silas down the hall. Security checked and approved the safety of the hospital floor. Employees glanced in his direction but quickly averted their eyes. His long-legged stride through the sterile space signaled his frustration. His aides walked a few feet behind him, waiting for a sign to come forward. The door to his godson's room opened as he approached.

His heart stuttered at the sight of bandages and machinery attached to the young man who was like a son to him. One of the greatest sorrows in his long life was his inability to reproduce. Cameron's parents had been his closest friends before his rise as Patron, and he'd promised to look after their son before they died in a tragic hunting accident

"Cameron," he lowered his voice as he spoke, not wanting to frighten the younger man.

At first, there was no response. Then a slight movement of his hand signaled he'd heard.

"Son, I am here. We will take you where you can recuperate faster. You need special care, Doctor Fields has already made the arrangements, you will be leaving soon." He moved closer and touched the young man's hand. The slight flinching beneath his confirmed Cameron heard and knew someone, if not him in particular, was with him. For the moment he had to be satisfied with that.

"We will discuss this attraction you have with dangerous situations when you are able. You promised to focus on a family, that means a mate, kids," whispering, he leaned forward. "Pups." He pulled a chair near the bed and sat, hand on top of the injured man's hand, and waited.

Within minutes, a gurney entered the room, and the transfer process started. "La Patron, may I have a word with you?" Dr. Fields asked with some hesitation and stepped backward.

Silas nodded.

"There is another case here that has caught my attention. I think you need to know about this one, there is an unregistered shifter –"

"He dies." Silas retorted. "You know the rules."

"I understand, but this is different. The shifter is unusual, he's a hybrid."

"A hybrid?" His brow rose, but his voice remained neutral.

"Yes Sir, I'm not sure what all the components are. Wolf shifter for sure, his mother and aunt are here. They are human, but their scents are not right. I've had their blood tested, and it's positive, she's his mother. What do you suggest I do?"

From the corner of his eye, Silas watched them load Cameron on the gurney while his mind latched onto the comments from the doctor. After living three centuries, a puzzle of any type was too difficult to ignore. "Let me see him, I should be able to identify his bloodline."

"Thank you, Sir," the doctor said, walking behind him and pointing to the room with the wounded man.

Cameron had received a private room. This soldier shared his space with other injured comrades. The stench of suffering and pain assailed Silas' sensitive nostrils, leaving a distinct metallic taste on his tongue. With little effort, he blocked out the other scents and focused on the lone male. As he stood near the door, the doctor spoke to the woman and gestured to the male on the bed.

The doctor nodded and walked toward him. Together they left the room.

"He is wolf, with a hint of another shifter. It's too small to determine the nature. What is his condition?" Silas asked frowning.

"He has fractures in his legs and arms, took a hit to his head and back. They'd pronounced him dead in Germany. He revived and is now here. He has had surgery on his arms and legs. They are trying to decide the next step for his head."

Silas shook his head. The possibility of discovery was too great. He wondered how much the human part of the young wolf had kept his dual nature from discovery so far. "Take him with you," he said.

The doctor nodded and left.

"Excuse me, Sir, excuse me." A small hand touched his arm before his guards could reach them. He stopped and looked at the brazen human woman. His brow lifted until she removed her hand. Things were becoming more and more interesting.

She stood around five-seven, weighed around one hundred forty-five pounds, with large breasts and wide, round hips. Her dark brown eyes and full lips were prominent features in her oval-shaped face. Her flawless creamy complexion, long, thick, black hair covered a side of her face and gave her an air of mystery. She was pretty in a willowy kind of way; unfortunately, she had no interest in men.

"I watched you talk to the doctor who's dealing with my nephew. Now the doctor wants to move him to another hospital. Why now? Why should my sister agree to this? Who are you?"

Silas couldn't remember anyone ever speaking to him in such an accusatory manner. His first remark would have been cutting. However, he remembered his recent pain at his godson's condition and decided to be civil. At least his version of civil.

He looked down at the woman and spoke in a clipped tone.

"According to the doctor, he has a similar condition to my godson who's being transferred for special treatment. Who I am is not important. And it's up to the military to decide what's in that soldier's best interest, not his mother. Don't forget, they own him." He turned and left her standing.

"Smug bastard," the woman whispered.

He waved his hand and kept moving.

Chapter 2

JASMINE BENNETT WALKED DOWN the hallway to her son, Tyrone's, room in the new facility. It was bigger, cleaner, and less crowded. When they'd arrived a couple of days ago, the sheer beauty of the facility had impressed her. The manicured lawn and what appeared to be acres of trees surrounded the red-bricked building with tall glass windows. Overall, the outside of the hospital offered a feeling of homiest. That impression lessened once you stepped inside. Modern equipment, doctors, nurses, and general hospital personnel filled the halls and rooms.

"Did you get any rest?" Renee, her older sister, asked, falling in step with her.

"About as much as you," she teased her sister. Neither had rested much since following the ambulance to this location. The nurse had offered them beds and a place to clean up, which they'd both utilized. Now, they waited while Tyrone underwent a series of tests.

"That much huh? Worried?" Renee asked as they turned a corner.

"Yeah, I know the doctor said he had slight brain damage, but Rone didn't seem too out of it to me yesterday. What did you think?" Jasmine asked as they entered his empty room.

Before Renee could say more, two huge orderlies wheeled Tyrone into the room. Both women stood and watched them transfer Tyrone from gurney to bed. The nurses checked the equipment and left with slight smiles.

"Rone, how you feeling sweetie?" Jasmine asked while gently

touching his swollen face. She ached seeing him like this and cursed the military that kept taking from her. Her baby was too young to fight.

He moistened his tongue. Renee picked up his cup and placed an ice chip on his lips.

"Umm, thanks, Aunty." His voice was just above a whisper.

"You're welcome. Now answer your mom. How are you feeling?"

"Like I've been blown up." He grimaced and chuckled.

Jasmine's hand flew to her chest as water filled her eyes. "Baby boy, I'm so sorry you're going through this. What —"

"Ma," he interrupted. "That was... horrible bedside humor on my part." His voice sounded stronger. "I'm feeling somewhat better. They've been treating me with meds that seem to be working. The nerve endings in my fingers and toes are healing." He moved the digits as proof. "All in all seems I will be around for a little while longer."

Jasmine broke down. Loud gushing sobs tore from her throat, her body shook as the fear of losing her son overcame her.

A nurse rushed into the room, checked the equipment, the patient, and then turned to Jasmine. Renee stroked her back as tears rolled down her face unchecked. The dam had broken with Tyrone's words. He looked better, but he had been on death's door just a few days earlier.

"She'll be okay," Renee said, her voice cracking. "She's just grateful he's recovering."

The nurse nodded, looked at them askance, and left the room.

"Mom... mom, I'm sorry. I didn't mean to worry you. I know you hate Rese and I joined the military after what happened to daddy. I can see this is too much for you." He paused as if to gain strength. "Aunty, why don't you take her for a ride, maybe she needs to get away from here for a little while."

"I'm not going anywhere," Jasmine countered, steel in her voice as she wiped her face with the back of her hand. "Yes, I hate the danger you and Tyrese are under in your line of work. As a mother, a part of my job description is to worry over my children. Your father loved what he did, and that made him who he was. I don't begrudge him that.

But never think for one second that because I disagree with your choices, I love you any less. It hurts me to see you in pain. You and your brother are my heart. That will never change, Rone. Never."

He nodded. A slight smile on his face. "Okay. The doctor should be here soon. I want to know his diagnosis. And you haven't called me baby boy since I was seven, thanks." He winked at her.

Her heart lifted at the small gesture. He was trying hard to convince her he was okay. She couldn't accept it, not after seeing him all bandaged up a couple of days ago. Granted, he looked much better now, but he *had* almost died. Had died and then revived. She was too grateful to take his recovery for granted.

Doctor Fields walked into the room looking over papers attached to a clipboard. "Someone wants answers I hear, let me see what we have." He paused, flipping the pages and reading. "Well, there's good news and not so good news here. First you, young man, are responding to the medications I have prescribed and are progressing very well. There is no apparent damage to your brain. Your back needs more work to insure no skeletal or nerve damage. If all goes well, we will start your treatment and therapy in three days. By then your legs and arms should be functioning enough to determine the extent of the damage to your back." He lifted kind eyes to Jasmine and then Tyrone.

"How long will all of this take, Doc?" Tyrone asked.

"It all depends on your arms and legs. If everything is the way I think, then about six to eight weeks. Maybe less."

"How is he healing so fast? What are you treating him with?" Renee, the skeptic, asked.

Jasmine hadn't thought about it before, but one of the doctors at the VA had said Rone would be down for months. They had been here for a couple of days and Tyrone showed remarkable signs of improvement.

"You aren't giving him experimental drugs are you?" Jasmine asked, voicing a new fear.

The doctor walked over to the IV and glanced at the writing before answering them. "No Ma'am, this hospital specializes in severe trauma cases, we have fewer patients and place all our energies on them getting better. Your son is in good hands." His soft-spoken words offered the comfort she desperately needed.

"Thank you," she murmured as he left the room.

"I'm glad you're doing better," Renee said while bending down to kiss his forehead.

"I'm glad you came, Aunty. It's good seeing you. Tell Mandy hi for me when you talk to her."

"You bet, speaking of which, I need to call her to check and see how the business is going. I'll be right back." She left the room, cell phone in hand.

"Mom, how long are you going to be here?" He looked out into the hall and then back at her.

"Until you're much better." She eyed him with determination. "Much better, so don't count on me leaving anytime soon."

He grinned.

His boyish smile wrenched at her heart. She longed to take him in her arms, hold tight and rock him like she'd done when he was little.

His smile fell away as he looked into the hall. She noticed and turned to look in the hall. It was empty. Frowning, she turned back to him.

The contemplative look on his face concerned her. "What is it?" She didn't mean to sound worried, it was just hard to sit back, helpless.

Shaking his head, he smiled. But this one didn't meet his eyes. "Nothing, just thinking about things. Have you heard from Rese?"

Recognizing the change of subject, she let it pass and answered. "Not yet. I left him a message and so did your Aunt. I hope to hear from him sometime today." A chill skittered down her back and she pulled her sweater closer. "Are you cold?"

"No, Ma'am. I'm warm." He picked up the remote.

Sitting back in the large, comfortable chair, she picked up her purse and pulled out her electronic reader. The earphones came out next. She didn't bother hiding her grin when he zeroed in on a drama television program. Slipping the earbuds into her ears, she turned on her reader and tuned out the noise in the room.

Engrossed in the story, she felt a chill down her arms. She glanced at Tyrone. He'd straightened on the bed and appeared to be at attention even though he lay on the bed. She frowned. Pulling out the earbuds, she started to ask him a question. That's when she heard someone's footsteps leaving the room.

Confused, she looked at him again. He stared at the door without blinking. Alarmed, she ran to the bed and shook him. It took a few shakes and yells before he blinked.

"Ma. It's okay. Don't cry. I'm okay." His voice lowered into a crooning sound. She had no idea she was crying. "I'm fine, just a little tired."

"But... but you didn't respond. It was like... like you didn't hear me." She sucked in a breath, hoping her trembling would stop. Her heartbeat wouldn't slow down and she tried not to become hysterical. But she'd never before seen him in a trance or whatever it was he'd been in.

He placed his hand over hers, looked her in the eyes, and spoke. "Mom, you're overreacting. I'm fine. It was nothing."

She jerked back as though he slapped her. "Are you... are you kidding?" She snatched her hand from his. "You must be joking. How the hell..." She stood up and walked off to the wall. *This boy just told me I was overreacting. He's lost his mind. Calm down?* Where was Renee?

"Ma?"

Without looking at him, she threw her arm back and held up her hand.

He remained quiet.

Closing her eyes, she inhaled and exhaled to slow her heartbeat. She visualized the boys when they were small. The twins had been a loving handful, but they'd filled her long days and nights. Now they were grown, and she was *overreacting*. She pushed down the anger that threatened to choke her.

Renee was right.

She needed to do something with her life. Maybe go back to school, take up a hobby, do something so she wouldn't overreact. Damn it.

She spun and stared at him. "I can't believe you said I overreacted."

He squirmed beneath the sheet. "Maybe that was the wrong word, but Ma, I'm okay. See?" He sat straighter.

"How the hell does that prove anything?" She hadn't meant to raise her voice, but he pissed her off and in a few minutes she *would* be overreacting.

The devilish grin he sprouted was reminiscent of when he was a young boy trying to escape punishment. "It doesn't. I just didn't know what else to say to keep you from going off on me."

She stared at him and started laughing. "You were close to the line. Don't do that. I want you to get well, not make you worse."

"Yes, Ma'am," he said in a meek tone.

"So what happened?" She returned to the side of the bed just in time to see his face shutter closed.

"Nothing. Just a daydream." He didn't look at her.

"Tyrone Bennett."

"Yes, Ma'am."

"You know the penalty for lying to your mama, right?"

He released a long, drawn-out sigh. "Yes. But I can't tell you."

"Why didn't you just say that? Do you think I'd try to make you tell me everything? You're grown and entitled to your secrets. Everybody got secrets. I'm concerned that's all."

"I'm sorry. I'm not up to par. Could you get the nurse in here, I need something for pain."

Her stomach dropped. "If I left you alone for a while would you still need the pain medication?" she asked in a soft voice.

"No." His voice rose, and then he gave her a sheepish grin as if afraid to admit he wanted his mama. "I'm glad you're here. My side is sore and I want to sleep. I can't do that without the drugs. Have you eaten?"

The change in topics threw her for a loop. "What?"

"Have you had anything to eat? You or Aunt Renee?"

She thought back and realized she hadn't had anything since early that morning. "I can't remember and I don't know about Renee. I'll ask when she comes back."

A few moments later, Renee and the nurse strode into the room.

The nurse stuck a needle into his IV and checked a few things. Jasmine noticed the nurse bend down and talk in a low voice with Tyrone. When they finished, the nurse turned, smiled at her and Renee, and left the room.

Jasmine itched to ask what the nurse said, but remembered her earlier remarks. "Is everything okay?" She stepped close to the bed and looked him over with a critical eye.

"Yeah, she wanted to know how bad the pain was." His eyelids drooped.

She gave into the urge to touch him, to reassure herself he was okay. The back of her hand stroked the side of his face. He sighed as he fell under the dominion of the medication.

"He's asleep?" Renee asked, coming to stand next to her.

Jasmine nodded, leaned down, and placed a kiss on his forehead. "Hungry?" she asked her sister.

"Yeah. You?"

Jasmine nodded as she backed away from the bed. "I am. Is there some place here where we can eat?"

"I think I overheard someone mention a cafeteria. I'll ask the nurse, and we can grab a bite before he wakes. Have you talked to the doctor about Tyrone's next step? It's good to see him healing, but what happens next?"

Jasmine hadn't asked that many questions because the doctor had been so forthcoming about Tyrone's condition. Before she could answer, Renee had walked off and was speaking to the nurse behind the counter.

"Thanks," Renee said to the nurse as she waved for Jasmine to meet her.

"There's a place here?" Jasmine asked as she caught up with her sister.

Renee nodded. "Yeah, a couple of floors down. Stairs or elevator?"

Jasmine looked toward the stairs but didn't feel up to it. "Elevator." Following the signs, they took the elevator and walked into the cafeteria. Scents teased her nostrils, her stomach growled. "I didn't realize how hungry I was before," Jasmine said, heading toward the line for the grill. There were steaks, burgers, and prime rib on the menu. Her brows rose at the choices. *No chicken or fish?*

Renee picked up a pre-made salad and waited for her.

"I'd like a steak, medium-rare. There needs to be a little pink in the middle. But I don't want a big steak."

The chef never spoke, he held up a raw piece of meat.

"Do you have anything smaller?"

He cut the steak in half and held it high.

Smiling, she nodded. "That's perfect, thank you." Jasmine stepped to the side and grabbed a small salad and garlic toast while waiting for her steak.

"What do you want to drink?" her sister asked.

"Water. A bottle, so I can take it back to the room."

"Good idea." Renee grabbed two bottles and picked up a large brownie.

"A salad and a brownie? How does that work out for you?" Jasmine teased as she accepted the plate with her steak from the chef. She slipped a tip in his jar and headed for the cashier. When they'd walked in the cafeteria earlier, it had seemed empty, but during the time they'd taken to grab their food, most of the tables had filled.

"Wanna sit outside in the sun?" Renee asked.

A table near the exit opened and Jasmine headed for it. The idea of swatting flies while trying to cut her steak held no appeal. "No, here's one." They each took a seat and looked out the large window. It was a beautiful day, maybe after they ate, she'd take a quick walk to stretch her legs.

"Jazz?"

"Hmmm?" She swallowed the garlic bread and took a deep breath. "Have you noticed there's a football convention going on here?"

"What?" She looked up at Renee.

"I mean, have you noticed how frigging big all the men are in this place? Even the women are tall. Plus there aren't any black people working here. We're in Maryland, how the hell can there not be any blacks working in a hospital."

Jasmine hadn't noticed the shape, size, or color of anyone. Her sole focus had been on Tyrone. She didn't care if the people were zebras. Tyrone was better, and that's all that mattered to her. But Renee was different. As an anthropology professor back in St. Louis, noticing people were her stock in trade.

"No. I hadn't noticed. I'm just glad Rone is getting better. Have you heard from Rese?"

Her sister cut her eyes at her. "No, I would've told you. And I'm glad they're taking good care of Rone, too. I owe them more than I can say. It's just weird being in a place so... so sterile. There's no diversity. Everyone's the same. Big men, tall women. All pale." Renee shivered. "It's just strange."

Jasmine looked out the window. Her eyes locked with a pair of turbulent bluish-green eyes. A chill snaked down her spine chased by a flash of heat. Her heartbeat stuttered and then picked up in speed. Warmth radiated through her and settled in her belly. A tingling started between her thighs. The alien feelings surprised her.

"See, they're big." Her sister tugged at her attention.

With reluctance, Jasmine pulled away from the fascinating eyes. "Huh?" A curl of warmth fluttered lower, tempting, and teasing.

"That guy you were looking at, did you see how big he was?"

She hadn't noticed anything but his eyes. "No, not really."

Renee sat back in her chair and stared at her. "That conversation we had back at the house a few days ago, you thinking about it?"

Jasmine fought through the fog clouding her mind. "No. Give me a minute to remember."

Renee chuckled. "Okay. What time do you want to head back to the room?"

"I'm not sure, Rone was in pain and the medicine helps him sleep." She finished eating and slid back from the table. "You want to take the scenic route back upstairs?"

Renee nodded as she joined Jasmine at the waste bin to dump their trash. Renee linked her arm in Jasmine's and headed toward the glass door leading to the gardens.

For the first time, Jasmine took note of the people in the room. The men were huge. It could've been a linebacker convention. She was glad when they walked out into the sun, but the clarity of those turquoise eyes haunted her.

Chapter 3

SILAS WATCHED THE HUMANS in the building walk arm in arm through the gardens. With half an ear he listened to another Alpha discuss plans for his pack. The Alpha was building a school on their land and was trying to find a way to keep it limited to just Pack.

"Make it private," one Alpha suggested.

"We did that and still had outsiders apply for enrollment," another Alpha said. "We found ourselves in a discrimination lawsuit and settled out of court. The laws are changing and it's harder and harder to be exclusive."

"But we have to allow a little interaction among humans. The problem is once that happens, friendships develop and all kinds of other things."

The Alphas mumbled their agreement.

Silas understood their dilemma. As their Patron and Alpha, he required each of them to stay current with the times. Pups were to be provided the best education, which spawned superior companies. Each Pack had to invest in real estate, and own their land. The members of the Pack were to be trained in either a trade or continue to college. The bottom line - all had to use their skills for the advancement of the Pack.

Unfortunately, there was a downside. The Packs under his leadership were vast, wealthy, and powerful. Their schools had the best academic programs, which provided the top test scores in their respective states. Humans wanted their children to attend those schools, but they couldn't allow the interaction.

"Why not say the schools are for the descendants of... your original Alpha, that would stop the lawsuits," Silas said into the silence.

"Yeah, that should work," Alpha Lyle, one of the attorneys present, said. "If the schools are built for a den, and it specified that purpose, it might work. But you may not be able to take part in state competitions."

"How many schools do we have in this country?" Silas asked.

"Over three hundred that comes to mind," Lyle said.

"Then plan our own academic competitions. Start at the state level, then regional, and then national. This way the barometer of academic excellence has greater meaning. Let's face it, the public schools offer no competition and the private schools are not that much better. But to pit a shifter school against another for scientific or mathematical excellence, that's a real contest. And I would judge on the national level," Silas said, knowing his involvement would settle the matter.

"That would be great. We can have all those who win your scholarships attend as well. That way they can extend their thanks as a collective voice," another Alpha said.

Pleased, Silas nodded as they discussed the change in the educational trajectory of their packs. Their energy and excitement was a tangible thing. For the most part, Silas acted as moderator, giving input when ideas became stalled. Each Alpha was responsible for his pack, and Silas was responsible for the Alphas who wore his insignia and carried his last name. Once the room quieted, Silas waited for the men to bring up what he felt was an obvious, urgent issue. Instead, they began discussing dinner destinations and frivolous pursuits for later that evening. Withholding a sigh, he reminded himself that these men concerned themselves with their individual State Packs. He bore the weight of broader issues affecting all wolves and had to bring them to the table.

"I wonder why no one has mentioned the humans on the grounds of this hospital," Silas said, looking around the room. The shocked expressions on the faces of the men who were responsible for thousands of lives were comical. He'd bet they still didn't see or understand his concern.

"What have I missed, La Patron?" Jayden, the Alpha for Maryland asked. The other Alphas sat forward with intense looks, prepared to remove any threat.

He looked at them and then spoke, sad that they still had not seen the challenge. "The mother of the shifter is human." He watched, waiting for them to get it. Some did, most did not. "The young wolf-shifter was not in our system and is an adult wolf who has changed on many occasions. He has a great relationship with his wolf. He has a twin, who is also a wolf. His mother is not, and she does not know her son is wolf."

The silence in the room was deafening. Frowns furrowed the brows of his Alphas. He could hear unspoken questions through their links.

"How is that possible?" One Alpha asked. "Wolves cannot mate with humans."

Silas nodded. "And yet a man lays in this facility. He is wolf. I have talked with him. His wolf acknowledges me. His father was a wolf, but not in a pack. It was his father who taught him and his brother how to change, and how to keep their wolf side hidden. The father was a military man and his sons followed in his steps. But the woman did give birth to them. This is not an adoption scenario; her blood runs in his veins."

No one spoke. Silas wondered how long before the importance of this discovery hit the Alphas.

"Well, damn," Jayden said.

"That about sums it up," another Alpha said.

"Could there be more?"

"Don't they need a pack? How did they survive without a pack?"

"Do they breed true?"

"Have they turned anyone?"

"Can they turn someone?"

"If we kill them, will that solve the problem?"

Questions swirled around the room, which was good for healthy discussion, but they had no answers. And that's what they needed.

Silas held up his hand. "Tomorrow at ten, schedule a test for the young wolf. Lyle will ask these questions and we will know more. We must separate him from his mother, she is over-protective and will take issue if we go to his room." He paused and met their gazes. "Indeed destroying the wolf, his twin, and his mother would solve a temporary problem, but how did it happen? I want answers, and so far, the young wolf and his family are the only ones who can give them. They die by my order alone."

The Alphas nodded.

Silas stood, and the Alphas stood, bowed, and filed out of the room. He sensed their disquiet and hoped for all their sakes the young man's answers filled in most of the blanks. But there was one question he couldn't answer. How had his mother carried not one, but two, pups to full term? She was an enigma, and even now his assistants performed a thorough background check on Jasmine Bennett and her family.

"A word, Sir?"

Silas turned and nodded to Lyle.

"Are there specific questions you want me to ask the young wolf?"

Silas nodded. "I will give you a list of questions in the morning."

Lyle nodded. "What is your opinion of him?"

Silas hesitated. His thoughts returned to the conversation he'd had with the young man earlier. His mother had sat in the chair listening with ear-buds to whatever was playing on her tablet. He was certain that was the only reason he'd been able to talk with the young wolf as long as he had.

"He has training, not pack training, so he might not be able to hunt with a pack. His father was in charge, but since his death, he and his brother have not chosen a pack. His father made sure they stayed on neutral territory and never had to declare an allegiance to anyone."

"Do you think he's open to having an Alpha?"

Silas shrugged. "I don't know. This one has Alpha potential, although he hasn't acted on it."

"That's good to know." Lyle bowed. "I will see you in the morning."

He turned and left Silas alone with his thoughts. While he'd been with the young wolf, he'd tried to discover if there was something special about his mother. He hadn't been able to pick up anything. Was she a rare treasured gift from the Goddess, or was she the first of many who could destroy his people? Her sons should not have been able to survive without a Pack. He could tell from her actions that she and her sons were very close. Even while he'd held the young man under compulsion, the thought of his mother being in danger threatened to break their connection. It wasn't correct to say the young wolf had no Pack. A better interpretation was he had no wolf-pack.

* * *

Silas sat behind the glass window in the training auditorium surrounded by at least thirty Alphas. Testosterone ran high in the small classroom, but it provided them the opportunity to watch Lyle ask the young wolf questions.

Once the young wolf understood he wasn't in the room for tests he'd sat up, hopped off the gurney, and sat in a chair. Silas silently applauded the young man's actions.

"My name is Tyrone Bennett, and I was born this way. My dad said it was because he and my mom had sex when he was just coming into his wolf. She got pregnant and had us." He shrugged as though it was no big deal.

"What's the name of your father's Pack?"

"I don't know, he never said. He had gotten a bad deal or something. We never met his parents or spent time with them. He didn't have anything good to say about Packs or his family."

"How did you keep this a secret from your mother? Or does she know you're a wolf?" Lyle asked.

The young man tensed. Silas could tell the question bothered him. "Dad made us swear never to tell anyone, including my mom. He said there were others out there who would hurt us or hurt her." His eyes narrowed. "No one hurts my mama." He paused. "Sometimes I think she suspects something is off a bit. Like during the full moon, my brother and I always left the house for camping trips or to hang with friends. Over time our excuses got real lame. She's smart, but she let it slide."

Silas nodded, taking a liking to the young man. He answered each question with open honesty. When Lyle finished, he asked the Alphas through their link if they were satisfied.

"I have a request," the young wolf said, startling everyone.

Lyle nodded.

"I want to see all the men who listened to our conversation if you don't mind."

Silas spoke through their link. *"That is fair."* All the men exited the small classroom. Silas was the last to enter. He met the young man's eyes and nodded.

"I understand this discussion was necessary. But I would like you to understand my mother and my aunt are here to make sure I'm okay. I have never told her about this part of my life. She's going to be pissed when I do." He shook his head and closed his eyes as though he dreaded that day. "But she loves me and I have to believe she'll forgive me. I don't want anything happening to her or my aunt. My mom's a special woman with a large heart. My dad told me she had to be kept away from others like us because they would try to take her. I can tell all of you," he stopped and shook his head. "Well not all, but most of you are mated, and that's not a problem, but some of the men working here have been giving her the eye and I can't protect her right now."

Silas frowned. The idea that this woman had to be protected from his males was a problem and one that shouldn't be on the table. "Are you saying she attracts unmated wolves?"

"That's what my dad said. Claimed he'd gotten into way too many fights. Although I suspect it was because his mate was a man and he seldom touched my mom."

Silas felt the jolt of disbelief flow through the Alphas. He straightened. "Your father married your mother, had pups and then turned her away to be with his mate?" *How was that possible*? Wolves bred with their mates; it had always been that way. This situation had serious repercussions.

The young man frowned in concentration. "I think mom and dad met in high school. My dad had just hit his change and was out of it for a while. I don't know about his relationship with his father, or why my dad was even around my mom at that time. They were just talking, nothing serious, but he lost control, they had sex and mom got pregnant. She was real young, sixteen. That's where things get blurry. My mom's parents were angry, but since both my mom and dad were underage, there wasn't a lot they could do. But my dad's parents disowned him or something drastic like that. He stayed in town, graduated early, and as soon as he was old enough, he joined the military and married mom."

There wasn't a sound after that bizarre tale. Silas could imagine how the wolf's family had responded to the information that a human girl was pregnant by their son. They wouldn't have believed it, but they should have reported it. That situation should never have been swept under the rug. He made a mental note to look into the life of this young man's father to discover the name of his pack.

"That is not normal," one Alpha said. Although his voice was gruff, he looked at the young wolf with compassion.

"No, it's not. What if this young wolf is not alone? What if more human women are capable of bearing our young?"

"What if these women can be mates?" The silence stretched unanswered.

Silas walked over to the young wolf. "Tyrone Bennett, your mother, and aunt are under my protection until you are well enough to reclaim that honor yourself. It speaks well of you to concern yourself of your female kin first. I will come by later today and you will introduce me. I ask that you hold off telling her of your dual nature, give us time to discover more about this unique situation. Also, continue to hold it close to yourself, tell no one of your father's concerns over his wife." Silas paused. "You said your father connected with his mate before his death?"

"When my father returned stateside, he took my brother and me hunting like he often did. Except this time, he introduced Matt as his mate. My brother took offense and fought both Matt and my father. I don't think either man expected that. After my brother wounded both men, he left. I stayed to help them get back to their car. My father begged me to understand the mate bond, but I had no point of reference. All I saw was my father cheating on my mom who had been faithful all those years. Everything changed after that. Whether it was guilt or what, I don't know. But my dad stayed away from home more and more. He gave the lamest excuses. Mom put on a brave front, but I could feel her pain and embarrassment. Tyrese, my brother, hated what my dad was doing and lost all respect for him. Matt and dad got a place in the next county. For a while, he tried to be a husband and a mate."

"Impossible, his wolf would never allow it," one of the Alpha's said.

"True, in the end, he lost it. He didn't want to hurt mom and he couldn't leave his mate. He never returned from his last tour."

Silas eyed the young man. "Do you think he lives? Perhaps he lives somewhere alone with his mate?"

The young wolf removed his hands from his head and crossed his arms. "Yeah. Yeah, I do. I guess he feels he's lived for everyone else, now it's his turn to live for himself."

Silas nodded, appreciating the young man's honesty, although he had to know they would have been able to smell a lie. "He left his wife's care to her sons. Under the circumstances that was probably for the best. She is free to continue her life without a man who is committed to another."

Although Silas had never heard of such a bizarre situation, he felt a pang of sympathy for them all. A mated pair had to be together or go insane. But the wife should've been taken care of, especially if she'd never agreed to become the wife of an unmated shifter. The boys had divided loyalties and that should never be the case. It was a mess that should have never occurred.

"Thanks, Tyrone," Lyle said, breaking the silence. "Your story stays between those of us in this room. We have a lot to think about and research. But we all wish you a speedy and full recovery. Our Patron has extended his protection, which means the protection of every Alpha who wears his crest. So be at ease and get well."

Silas noticed the young man's brow crease at the mention of the Patron. The Alphas left the room. "Who will take him back to his room?" Silas asked.

"I promised to call an orderly." Jayden looked at Tyrone. "Do you need help to lie down?" He patted the top of the gurney.

"No." Tyrone walked over and sat on top. He looked at Silas. "Thank you. I don't know what a Patron is. I hope you can help fill in the missing blanks in my education."

Cameron hadn't recovered well enough to be moved to Silas' home yet, so he intended to be in the area a while longer. Perhaps he'd move Cameron and Tyrone to Jayden's lands, where they could control security better. He'd think about that.

"Sure. Go now and put your mother's mind at ease. You've been away for a while." Silas touched Tyrone on the neck. The young man fell asleep. He backed up as the orderlies came in and wheeled him out.

Jayden waited but didn't speak.

"He needs to rest and we need the time to check out his story." He glanced at Jayden and Lyle, who nodded. They left the room. Silas hoped Tyrone's story was wrong, but he doubted it. No matter how he cut it up, he smelled trouble headed in their direction.

Chapter 4

JASMINE STOOD AS THE orderlies wheeled Tyrone into the room, and watched as they laid his limp body on the bed. The nurse followed and hooked him up to the IV. A hand rested on her shoulder. "He's out of it, huh?" Renee said.

Jasmine nodded.

"You want to grab a bite to eat?"

Jasmine shook her head. "No. I'm not hungry right now. Go and get you something. I'll be right here." She retook her seat and stared hard at her son. There was a niggling feeling in the back of her neck that something was skewed. He looked drugged. She looked at the IV and realized that was a possibility. Leaning forward, she rested her fist beneath her chin and looked around the large room. Everything in this place was plus-sized, made for big people like her sister said. She chuckled at the absurd thought.

Her cell rang, and she dug it out of her bag, checking to make sure the noise didn't bother him. Her heart pounded with profound relief when she looked at the caller ID.

"Rese? Rese how're you doing, sweetie?" Her throat tightened when she heard the deep timbre of his voice. Her boys were now men.

"I'm okay, Mom. I got your message, where's Rone?"

"He just came back from tests and he's asleep now. But it was close for a minute." She didn't want to get into everything with him being so far away, but she knew he wanted to know.

"I know. It was… well, it was weird. I felt him leave. It freaked me out and almost cost the lives of my unit when I fell flat on my face. They said I was unconscious for five minutes."

Her hand flew to her mouth in horror. "Oh my God," she whispered, closing her eyes. This was too much. Both her sons had been at risk. She frowned. How was that possible?

He released a long sigh. "I'm being sent back for testing. My commander doesn't want to risk me passing out again. I'll be stateside, Bethesda in twenty-four hours. I had to wait to call you until I got clearance."

Her heart ached for him. "Are they putting you out of the service?" She knew how much he enjoyed his work. She didn't like it or understand why he courted danger, but she tried to be supportive.

"I'm not sure. The connection with Rone isn't my fault or something within my control. But when he winked out, he took me on a ride with him. That's never happened before now. Maybe with these tests, they'll figure out something."

On one hand, her heart ached for him, but on the other, she was jumping for joy that he'd be here tomorrow. She'd have both her boys. "We're at another hospital, one that specializes in the trauma Rone had. Whatever they're doing for him, it's working. When we got here a few days ago, he looked like he was on his last leg. Now, he sits up, talks, and eats. I don't know why that doctor at the other military hospital said it would take him months to recover."

She heard his breath whistle through the phone. His silence concerned her. "Rese? Rese, he's going to be alright. I'll tell him you're coming and that'll cheer him up. Don't worry, he'll be fine."

"Ma... Ma, I..."

"Yeah, baby?" She waved over her sister, who was holding a tray of food.

"I love you and can't wait to see you."

She smiled. "I love you, too. Your aunt just walked in, say hello." She held the phone out to her sister, picked up a fried pickle from the plate, and popped it into her mouth.

Renee squealed. "I can't wait to see you, Boo. You sound good and have just made my day."

Jasmine looked up and noticed a handsome man standing near the entrance. He wore sunglasses. His thick dark hair was brushed back from a widow's peak. As he stepped into the room, her eyes roamed across his wide chest, flat, narrow stomach, and long thick legs. The short-sleeved shirt he wore stretched taut across his chest and protested the large muscular arms pulling at the seams. He wore a tailored pair of dress pants and dark leather loafers.

A tingling started at the base of her neck, slid down her back, and settled in her core. Her face warmed when she realized he'd been watching her stare at him.

"Can I help you?" she asked, pulling her eyes to his face. High cheekbones, a straight nose, full firm lips, and nice teeth. She couldn't see his eyes but was sure they enhanced his looks alongside everything else. He wasn't pretty. Two words came to mind, masculinity personified. One hundred percent all man.

"I came to check on Tyrone. I met him earlier this morning, and he asked me to stop by later to meet his mom and aunt."

"Oh." She looked at Tyrone who was stirring, but not fully awake, and then at the man who had to be almost six and a half feet tall. They sure grew them big out here.

"Sir?" Tyrone whispered, struggling to sit forward.

All thoughts of a sexy man flew out of her mind as she walked to Tyrone's bed and fluffed his pillow. The tall male followed.

Renee eyed him and pointed at his back. "That's him. That's the one," she mouthed.

The man turned to look at Renee. She handed Jasmine the phone and walked to the other side of the bed. "How you feeling, Rone? Do I need to call a nurse?" Renee asked, avoiding looking at the handsome stranger.

"No, just a few ice chips, please."

"Sure." She picked up the bucket, shook a small amount of ice into his cup, and placed one on his lips.

Eyes closed, his head flopped back. "How long have I been out?"

"Just a couple of hours," Jasmine said, looking over her shoulder at the silent giant. "You have a visitor, someone other than me and your aunt."

His eyes opened and she could have sworn they flashed. But it happened so fast she wasn't sure. "Rone?"

He turned his gaze to her.

"What's wrong?"

"Nothing. I'm just waking from a deep sleep. I think the meds were too strong, I shouldn't have been out that long." Although he was talking to her, he kept looking at the guy behind her.

"Should I call a nurse, have her check it out?"

"No, I'll talk to the person in charge to make sure that doesn't happen again."

There was a grunt behind her. She spun around, and the man looked down at her. Sticking out her hand, she introduced herself. "Hi, I'm Jasmine Bennett, Tyrone's mom."

He took her hand. "I'm Silas Knight, an administrator of this facility."

"Why didn't you just say that when were in the first hospital?" Renee asked, her tone testy.

He shrugged and released Jasmine's hand. He stepped forward and spoke to Tyrone. "How are you feeling right now? Rested?"

Nodding, Tyrone looked at the man for a second or two. "But I might take the doctor up on the therapy tomorrow." He said it as if it were an afterthought.

"What time tomorrow?" Jasmine asked, frowning. She didn't know how much time Tyrese would have to spend with them and she didn't want Tyrone to miss him.

"Uh... I don't know." He glanced up at Silas. "I guess I can ask the doctor in the morning."

Jasmine eyed their visitor and spoke. "Good. Rese called while you were out."

"He did?" A light flared in her son's eyes.

Jasmine nodded, so pleased with his response she forgot the

stranger. "Yeah. He should be here tomorrow."

"Tomorrow?" Tyrone beamed. Then he frowned. "Are you sure? How'd he get leave?" His eyes slid to Silas and then returned to her.

Hesitating, she bit her lip, not wanting to talk about family business in front of a stranger.

"We'll talk about that later," Renee said. "Silas, do you know how long they intend to keep my nephew here? Can he be transferred to St. Louis and receive treatment there?"

"That is something we can discuss with the doctor in the morning. I'm not exactly sure what therapy is planned for Tyrone, so I cannot say."

"Thanks." Renee nodded and turned back to Jasmine, her brow raised.

"Something smells good." Tyrone lifted to see over the footboard.

Jasmine looked back at the tray with quite a few goodies on it. "Your aunt brought back lunch, but none for you until the doctor clears it."

His face fell as he slumped back on the bed. "Tomorrow. I need real food to get better."

She and Renee laughed.

Silas smiled. He had a nice smile, Jasmine thought.

"Mom, Aunt Renee, I wanted both of you to meet Silas Knight. He's the top man in charge."

Silas looked at her and then Renee. "If you need anything or have any concerns, feel free to come to me."

"How do we contact you?" Renee asked.

With an economy of movements, he handed Jasmine a card, nodded at Tyrone, and walked out of the room.

When she could no longer hear his footsteps, Jasmine sat on the edge of the bed and held Tyrone's hand.

"Now that's a man." Renee blurted.

Both Tyrone and Jasmine stared wide-eyed at her.

"What? Because I prefer women don't mean I can't appreciate a good-looking man. I do. I just don't want to do more than look."

"Okaaay," Jasmine said, turning from her smirking sister and looking down at Tyrone. "Rese is being sent stateside for testing. When you…" She couldn't say died. "Went under, he fainted in the middle of a tense situation."

Tyrone's eyes widened.

"It… it caused a problem for his unit." She swallowed hard, feeling him tense. "So he's being sent back for testing and to see if he can still serve in the military." She watched as his eyes closed tight. His head fell to the side away from her. Wary, she sought Renee to get her take on what she'd said.

Her sister shrugged. "They've always been close. I imagine this separation has been hard for each of them. Maybe they have to serve together."

Jasmine shook her head. "Rese is Marines."

Her sister frowned.

"Rone is Army."

"Oh. I got it. Can't mix the two." Renee brushed Rone's cheek. "It's going to be okay, your brother will be here tomorrow and the two of you can work it out." She looked at Jasmine. "With Rese here, chances are they'll both have to do some psyche stuff."

Jasmine nodded, she hadn't thought about that. But it didn't matter, there was no place other than right here she needed to be. She'd paid off her house. Her few bills were on automatic bill pay. Her car remained safe in her garage and her mail sat at the post office. Plus she had great neighbors who looked out for one another.

"Probably, but we'll get it all worked out."

Tyrone turned and looked at her for a few moments. He squeezed her hand and lifted up on the bed. "Ma," he whispered and fell into her arms.

Rubbing his face and back, she whispered. "It's going to be okay, Rone. You'll see. Things have a way of working out. You'll see." She kept rocking him until his tense muscles relaxed, and he kissed her on the cheek. He reached for his aunt. She leaned over him and held him close for a while.

"Your mama's right, Rone. Things always work out in the end. We don't understand everything, but we have one another and we stick together."

He nodded. When he looked up at her again, his eyes were uneasy. With the threat of his brother being put out of the service, and him as well, he had a right to be troubled. So she let him be. But her gut churned in apprehension.

They'd always been able to fix problems by meeting them head-on. As a single parent, for the most part, she'd had to think outside the box and many times, create a whole new box. But this was the government and her influence was non-existent. Her husband had spent almost twenty years serving Uncle Sam, but she had never met any of his unit or any of his friends. He'd kept her separate from his career. They'd never lived on base. From the very first, he'd always rented a house far away from town and base.

She pulled herself from the dark muddle of yesterday. "That's right, Sis."

Chapter 5

SILAS MOVED DOWN THE hall, deep in thought. There was something about Jasmine Bennett that attracted his wolf. Not only did that surprise him, but it also pissed him off as well. The attraction wasn't just superficial, not that she wasn't an attractive woman, she was quite beautiful. Smooth, creamy fair skin, a nice firm body, and an even nicer smile. She was a little taller than her sister and her breasts and hips were larger. He closed his eyes to stop dissecting her. She was a sexy statuesque package with curves in all the right places. Her body and face would attract any human, but shouldn't pull a wolf, especially his.

And that was the problem.

His wolf had stirred and sniffed, curious of her unique smell. Tyrone had picked up the energy and asked him what was going on through their link. Silas had no idea and waited to see what his wolf was going to do. While they were in the room, his wolf seemed content to watch, but the fact that a human stirred his wolf for the first time in centuries concerned him.

Jayden met him at the door of the conference room. All the Alphas had waited to hear his report. He sat and looked at the earnest expressions in the room.

"We have a problem."

Silence greeted his announcement.

"My beast stirred and observed the woman. That has never happened before with a human female. I understand Tyrone's concern.

She will draw the attention of unmated males."

"How has she survived this long?" one of the Alphas asked.

Lyle opened a file. "Her husband always made sure they lived in neutral areas where there weren't any Packs. She was a housewife, didn't go out much unless it was for her sons. The home she lives in now is in an area without a Pack. She travels to St. Louis once a year and stays with her sister who is a lesbian living with her lover Mandy Ashford. I doubt they go places where a male would catch her scent."

"Talk about the protection of the Goddess," another Alpha said.

"My thoughts exactly," Silas said, looking at the Alphas. "We have to be very careful with her. No harm can fall her way."

"What about the sister?"

Silas thought back. "My wolf ignored her. I don't know if that means she does not attract wolves or that my wolf showed interest in the more dominant of the two. Tyrone's mother is strong."

"Strong?"

"Very strong-willed, like an alpha bitch," Silas said, paying her the highest compliment.

The men nodded.

"What next? We know Tyrone didn't lie, and he has asked for the protection of his mother and aunt, which you granted. Do we search for the father to get answers? Or put out feelers to see if this has happened before? Or just assume she's the one gift from our Goddess?" Jayden asked.

"I want this contained," Silas answered. "No one talks about it or asks questions yet. We can't afford to put any humans at risk. We have a full-functioning wolf, born and raised by a human. Can you imagine the fallout? A lot of wolves would begin looking at humans again to breed." He shook his head. "I want this muzzled. But keep your ears and eyes open. I agree with Tyrone, the father and his mate are probably in another state or country, living together. We'll keep him dead as long as an emergency doesn't arise."

Jayden held up a file. "I have the information on his father's former Pack. You were right, they tossed him out once he stood by the girl he impregnated. He refused to say she was lying. The pack is in Oklahoma. Should we contact them?"

Silas thought for a few minutes. "Not right now, but it's good knowing the history of the twins. And by the way, Tyrese will be here tomorrow. Seems when Tyrone died, he pulled his brother down with him. It was right in the middle of a mission. He's being sent here for evaluation."

"His military career is over," one of the Alphas muttered.

"Pity Uncle Sam can't see the value of having two connected twins working for them," Silas smirked.

The alphas smiled as they nodded.

"I see them as a tremendous asset to our nation, but we'll see how the evals turn out." He looked around the room. "Who's on watch tonight?"

One of the Alphas spoke. "I've got two men in the hall and two stationed outside to follow them if they leave."

Silas nodded. "Good." He waited until everyone had left, and walked back toward Tyrone's room. The closer he got, the more his wolf strained and whined for contact. There was no answer, or response. That should have upset his wolf, but he didn't sense that. When he reached the hallway, he nodded to the guards. When he started down the hall he'd had no intention of entering the young wolf's room, but found himself striding forward. He sent a silent greeting to the man on the bed, informed him about the guards, and wished him a good night.

"*Thank you, Sir,*" the wolf said through their bond.

Silas nodded and glanced around the room. He'd heard the woman's sounds of sleep when he reached the door, yet he needed to see her for himself. His wolf quieted until he left the room.

With each step, his wolf whined and became agitated. Silas stopped and looked back toward the room. His wolf eased up, it was obvious that he wanted to return. Deep in thought, he and his security detail left for Jayden's pack lands to spend the night.

***

"Welcome, La Patron," Jayden and his mate, Maureen, greeted him as he entered their home.

He nodded, kissed her cheeks, and clapped Jayden on the shoulder. "It has been a long time Maureen, but you are still as exquisite today as you were thirty years ago when you married this scamp."

She blushed to the roots of her dark brown hair. Green eyes and a pert upturned nose graced strong, high cheek bones in an oval-shaped face. "Thank you, La Patron." She bowed in submission.

"We have prepared your rooms," Jayden said, stepping back and waving to the staircase. "Your things are there already."

"Good," Silas said as he followed the couple through the long hall. "Where are your pups?" he asked, not scenting the children.

Maureen glanced back at him. "They are at a sleep-over birthday party next door but will be back in the morning. You get a night's rest without them climbing all over you." She smiled.

Since the couple knew how much he enjoyed playing with the pups, he nodded. "I will see them before returning to the hospital tomorrow. I have a surprise for them. He didn't give gifts to his hosts though he always brought a gift for their children. It was important for the pups to know him as someone who looked out for them and not a mysterious old man who ruled from afar.

"They will enjoy that. Thank you for honoring our home with your presence and let me know if you need anything." Maureen dipped her head and walked off, leaving Silas and her mate in the suite of rooms set aside for him.

"On the surface, this seems like a small thing," Silas said. He pinched the bridge of his nose before moving to the desk in the corner of the room. "But I sense a lot more." He sat at the desk and booted up the laptop from his briefcase.

"If you think there's more, there is more. I trust your instincts." Jayden said with confidence as he stood near the desk.

Silas wished he was as confident as the Alpha sounded. A niggle of worry slid through him at the anomaly. A human who gave birth to his kind presented all types of challenges. The need to get a handle on the complication buffeted him.

"I'm going to check a few things." He typed in a variety of passcodes until he reached an encrypted site. Very few beings knew the site existed, a series of wards guarded its access.

After running numerous searches, he came up empty. Frustrated, he blew out a breath and raked his hand through his hair. "Damn."

Jayden watched but remained silent.

"So far nothing," Silas said, leaning back in his chair. There had been no predictions, no forewarning, no myths or legends that mentioned humans being able to procreate with wolves.

Jayden nodded.

"We will continue the search for information. An unmated bitch with the ability to breed and no connection to Pack is not a good thing."

Jayden nodded. "I agree. Add to that she has no idea what's going on, and that could be a door for human authorities to enter."

Outside of Tyrone's mother, Silas wasn't that concerned about the humans right now. He was curious of the underlying reason for a human breeder in their midst. He'd lived too long to believe in coincidences. "What if I missed the call about Cameron?" He stared at Jayden trying to make sense when there was none. "Why weren't the twins flagged when they joined the military? Are they that good at hiding?"

"Only Alphas and you are that good," Jayden said.

"That's my point," Silas said, tapping the desk. "They've no training to use that skill, yet they have lived twenty years avoiding detection."

"I'm sure it was because of the severe injuries we discovered them at all," Jayden said.

"We need to see what capabilities these wolves have. Secure lodgings for the twins and their mother on your grounds. They will need to be our guests for a while longer. I want security on them at all times. There are still too many unanswered questions and we need more time to uncover the mystery." Plus he suspected their connection was unique and wanted to watch them further.

"Yes, Sir."

Silas stood and stretched, ready to be alone with his thoughts. "I'm going to make arrangements to send Cameron to my home; Jacques will take care of him as well as the Alpha trainees a little longer while I work on this problem. Go to sleep; we'll start fresh in the morning."

Jayden nodded and walked toward the door. "Rest well."

"You too." Silas watched the door close behind one of his favorite Alphas. Jayden suffered abuse as a pup. Cast aside by his pack because he lacked a finger on his left hand. It was obvious to Silas the man had the heart of a warrior, but his paw caused him problems at times. Not that it stopped others from following his leadership. By the time Silas met Jayden, the pack leader had over twenty wolves following him. Impressed with the man's integrity and desire to insure his pack received the best he could give them, Silas offered him the opportunity to train as one of his Alphas. Jayden's man's first concern was for his pack during his absence, as it should have been. Silas installed the beta as a temporary leader while Jayden went through months of training required to be a La Patron Alpha.

Silas had never repented of his decision. Before preparing for bed, he rebooted the laptop, there was one other site he wanted to check. While waiting for it to come online, he stripped off his shirt and laid it across the brocade-covered chair.

He glanced at the mirror across the room and grimaced. It had been a long day, and he looked like a wet mutt. No doubt Jacques, his servant, would be horrified to see the five o'clock shadow on his angular jaw. He rubbed the scratchy surface as he realized the blinking cursor awaited his next instruction. He typed in the website, pleased with the number of hits.

He chose the first and read the contents, even going so far as to verify the footnotes. Two and a half hours later, concern had turned to dread. As he continued reading, the dread magnified into fear. The ancient strategy slapped him in the face, infuriating him.

The kingdom of heaven is like what happened when a farmer scattered good seed in a field. 25 But while everyone was sleeping, an enemy came and scattered weed seeds in the field and then left.26 When the plants came up and began to ripen, the farmer's servants could see the weeds. 27 The servants came and asked, "Sir, didn't you scatter good seed in your field? Where did these weeds come from?"28 "An enemy did this," he replied. His servants then asked, "Do you want us to go out and pull up the weeds?" 29 "No!" he answered. "You might also pull up the wheat. 30 Leave the weeds alone until harvest time. Then I'll tell my workers to gather the weeds and tie them up and burn them. But I'll have them store the wheat in my barn."

Furious with the possibility that an enemy had set a nefarious plan in motion to infiltrate and weaken the wolves with half breeds he opened the window and leapt to the ground. The moment he touched the soil, his paws dug into the cool earth.

The need to reconnect with nature thrummed through him. He ran through the complex and out into the forest surrounding the compound, the dark blue-black coat of his wolf almost invisible in the night.

Anxious, his wolf recognized the inherent threat to his pack and wanted to attack. The man in him realized the need to allow his wolf the freedom to run but cautioned the cunning beast of the need to plan as well as protect. They'd get in front of the threat before things spiraled out of control.

After a long, exhilarating run, Silas returned to the house. Jayden had left the back door open. Still in wolf form, he padded up the stairs to his room. Once in the room, he shifted and closed the door behind him. A shower was his next order of business.

Afterward, he walked downstairs to make sure he secured the door and discovered all traces of the debris he'd tracked in from his late-night run was gone from the floor.

The softness of his bed called out to him as he retraced his steps, and he fell into a troubled sleep.

Chapter 6

JASMINE WALKED INTO TYRONE'S room, well-rested, yet uneasy over the speed of her son's recovery. Her sister may have a point, she thought, looking over her shoulder at the large man in the hall who watched her and then turned when he noticed she'd seen him. Was he following her? She frowned at the idea and walked inside the room.

The doctor stood at the bed talking with Tyrone in quiet tones. When she entered, her son smiled at her.

"Good morning, Mrs. Bennett," the doctor said, reaching for her hand.

"Morning." She placed her bag in the lower drawer and turned to face them.

"You look pretty," Tyrone said.

"Thanks, hon." She placed a kiss on his brow and looked at the doctor who watched them.

"What's next for him?" she asked with a touch of apprehension.

The doctor's brow furrowed as though he hadn't expected that question. After clearing his throat he looked down at her. "I was just discussing that with Tyrone. I'm pleased with the progress of his healing." His face pinked. "Although he needs more rest for a complete recovery," he rushed, almost as an afterthought.

She eyed him and looked at her son.

"I have him scheduled to move to a rehab complex in the city for more treatment, and—"

Jasmine's hand flew up in the air. "Hold up." She pointed at the doctor, who appeared shocked at her interruption. "Seven days ago, my son stopped breathing, was in critical condition. The doctor told me it would take months for him to recover and now, he's been here, what – five days, and almost looks like he did before he left for this last deployment." She inhaled, pulling her thoughts together. "Now, I don't want you to think I'm not grateful." She shook her head. "I am, but something's not right. Tell me right now what treatment you've given him that has him like this." Her stomach quivered with nerves. She prayed they hadn't done experimental procedures on her boy.

"Mrs. Bennett, the treatment I used on your son is a patented process unique to our hospital. It works when the recipient is in top condition and can heal on his own with therapy." He crossed his arms and looked down at her. "I assure you, Tyrone has received the best medical care in the country for his situation."

She crossed her arms. "Explain why the doctor at the other hospital said it would take so much longer for him to heal."

He shrugged, nonplussed. "I can't answer that. But I will tell you we use cutting-edge technology here that many hospitals in the area don't. And I am an expert in my field. We have done nothing wrong here." He finished his tirade in a huff.

Exasperated that he'd put her on defense, she backed off, unwilling to apologize for being a concerned parent, but recognizing the need to mend bridges. Instead of addressing the specifics of Tyrone's care, she ventured down another path. "Is this place expensive? Will the Army cover the cost?" No one had asked her for any information on him and that struck her as strange.

His face tightened. "Mr. Bennett has already talked to finance and admissions. From what I've read, his financial arrangements are current."

She looked at her son. His clenched jaw stopped the next remark from leaving her mouth. Had she gone overboard? Embarrassed him? She wasn't sure.

"Sorry I'm late," Renee said, strolling into the room. She stopped and looked between the three occupants in the room. "What happened?"

Jasmine glanced at her son. The muscle in his forehead jumped. "Nothing, the doctor was just saying he wants Rone to go to another facility to finish recuperating."

Renee eyed the doctor and then walked over to her nephew. "Rone, honey?"

He opened his eyes half-mast. "Hi, aunty."

"Hey, sweetie. How do you feel? Are you up to moving again?" Worry clear in her voice.

Tyrone nodded. "I feel good, but I need to get stronger. Food, exercise, and time should do the trick."

Renee patted his shoulder as she glanced at Jasmine. "When did you want him to begin?" she asked the doctor.

"By the end of the week, he should be ready by then."

"Will there be a place for my sister?" Renee asked. "I'm leaving later today, things came up and I need to get back to Missouri. My other nephew will need to crash there as well."

The doctor nodded, a pensive look on his face. "Living quarters are available for those using the facility because people come from all over the country." There was a thread of pride in his voice. "I'll check on what's available and get back to you." He made a point of looking at Tyrone when he said that last bit.

Jasmine stewed as they discussed her son's next move as though she weren't standing in the room. Did they want to play this card? She fumed as she listened.

"Okay, when's Rese getting here?" Renee asked, looking at Tyrone and then at Jasmine.

Tyrone shrugged. "I don't know, do you, mom?"

It was on the tip of her tongue to lash out, but she resisted and shook her head instead. Rather than explode over her treatment, she picked up her purse, hefted it onto her shoulder, and left the room without a backward glance. She'd made it to the lobby when her cell beeped.

Inhaling, she spoke in a calm tone. "Hey, baby. Where are you?" she asked Tyrese while pushing open the heavy glass door and then walking into the gardens.

"I'm just finishing up my debriefing. I'm waiting for my driver and then heading over there. How's Rone?"

"He seems to be doing better, the doctor wants to move him to another facility for therapy and stuff," she said, wondering what he thought of the move. He knew better than anyone how serious Tyrone's injury had been.

"He does? Hmmm. What do you think about that?"

She released a long pent-up breath. "First off, I'm surprised by how fast he's healing. Don't get me wrong, if I never see him look the way he did that first day, I'm okay with that. It's happening so fast. When I asked the doctor about it, he got offended and Rone acted like I'd embarrassed him."

"For real?" The surprise in his voice was a soothing balm to her injured feelings. It had always been the three of them against the world. She understood they were able to make their own decisions, but there had always been respect and love between them.

"Yeah." The sadness in her voice must have translated through the phone.

"Mom, you know he'd never do anything to stress you out. He's going through things right now, don't let it get to you."

She looked straight ahead at the wild array of brilliant colors in the garden, inhaled the multitude of fragrances, and allowed the sweet smell to ease her pain. "Hmmm."

"Where are you?"

"What?"

"Where are you right now?"

"I'm at the hospital."

"With Rone?"

"No."

"Okay. Tell me, where you are?"

"Sitting in the garden."

"Garden?"

"At the hospital. It's pretty, and it calms me."

"Okay. I'm in the car now and should be there in about…" he paused. She heard him talking to someone, ten more minutes. I want to see you first. Can you wait for me in the garden, please?"

Jasmine looked up at the cloudless blue sky. Throughout most of her marriage, her husband ignored her. The one thing she'd counted on keeping her sane was the connection with her sons. Now that appeared to be waning.

A shaft of pain lodged in her chest. "Yes, I'll wait. See you soon." Weary, she disconnected and pulled a stick of gum from her purse. "What the hell happened to me?" she murmured. She'd met Davian in high school, they'd become friends. One night he'd been in pain and had come to see her. He couldn't speak, he hurt so bad. Something clicked inside her and all she wanted was to ease his suffering. Instead of following her parent's rule of no company when they weren't at home, she'd allowed her friend to come in for just a few minutes.

He'd looked terrible.

Sweat dripped from all over his body. One minute he'd been hot, the next cold. It baffled her, and she had no idea what to do. She held him as he cried, jerking in pain. Later, his breathing normalized and when he could speak, he thanked her. She'd pushed away, but he'd grabbed her hand and kissed her.

At first, she'd struggled, but the timid boy who'd been her closest buddy turned out to be really strong. One thing led to another and the next thing she knew, she'd cried out in pain and tried to push him off her. He moved a few more times, grunted, and rolled off. She'd scrambled away from him and demanded he leave. He started crying and apologizing as she pushed him out the door.

Two months later she told him she was pregnant. Her life had been one of duty and doing the right thing. Davian never loved her, and she didn't love him either. But she'd been pregnant with twins. It hurt her parents. They wanted her to give her children up for adoption. Davian's parents had been assholes and disowned him when he owned up to his kids. It had been hard in the beginning. She'd never made it to college as she'd dreamed. The constant moving and living in the boonies kept her from making lasting friendships. Now, at thirty-six, she was alone, and that sucked.

Tyrese Bennett hung up the phone and ground his teeth in anger at his brother. The one person they'd both swore would never be hurt in this charade was their mother. She'd suffered years of neglect and emotional abuse from their father. Although they'd promised their old man to never expose their wolf nature to anyone, keeping that bit of information from their mom hurt the most. His dad had been adamant that they keep her in the dark for her safety, but he'd never bought into that explanation.

Heaven help them if she ever discovered they'd kept the fact their father had found his mate and had lived the last few years of his life with Matt. Tyrese had hated the way his father treated his mom and vowed to never give her cause to be sad again. Now she sat in the gardens of that hospital upset because she had no idea her son was a wolf with serious healing capabilities.

He reached out to Tyrone through their link. *"What'd you do to Mom?"*

"Hello to you too, bro."

"Answer me." Tyrese wasn't in the mood to play games. Tyrone knew how protective he'd become of their mother since his dad had proved how much of an ass he could be.

"She was questioning the doctor over my care like I was an idiot just laying here. I didn't say anything to her—"

"You're an ass."

"Of course I am. And you are?"

"Think for one moment how she feels. You were dead. Get that? Dead a week ago; now you're ready to go jogging. She doesn't understand your wolf abilities. Humans do not heal that fast."

"Damn."

"Yeah. If she's upset, I swear I'm gonna fuck you up."

"Too late, that's already happened. I'll send Aunty to find her so I

can apologize."

"I got this. I'll see you later." Tyrese disconnected their mental link as the car pulled beneath the hospital portico.

"Thanks, man." He passed the driver a few bills as he exited the car. Striding inside to the information desk, he ignored the curious glances. "Hi, which way to the garden?"

"Which one? We have three," the lady at the counter said, as she pulled a map from her desk. Pointing at the diagram, she spoke. "This is the largest, and it's near the cafeteria." Her finger roved the sheet. "And the other two smaller ones are located here and here. Just follow the map and signs, you shouldn't have any problems."

He took the paper and noticed she'd written a phone number on the front. He sent her a wink and a smile, with a promise in his eyes to get back in touch. It had been a while since he'd indulged himself between a woman's thighs, and she looked hot.

"I need to talk with you. Come to my office." Tyrese stumbled as an unfamiliar voice entered his mind. At first, he thought he was hearing things. He looked up and then around, searching for speakers. When he didn't see anything, he shrugged and continued toward the cafeteria gardens.

"I'm not going to ask you again. Come into my office, now."

This time there was no way Tyrese could misunderstand. Someone had just spoken to him through a similar link he'd used to speak to his brother a few minutes ago. Curious and half afraid, he followed the thread.

"Who are you?"

"La Patron. I need to speak to you before you speak with your mother."

At the mention of his mother, Tyrese balked. *"My mom? What does she have to do with this?"* One moment he was standing in the middle of the hall, the next he was on all fours in wolf form.

He yelped. His paws all but slid over the concrete floor as the feeling of being dragged forward ran through him. His wolf followed directions that led him up a series of stairs into a room where two men sat at a conference table.

"Close the door," a large man with green eyes said.

Tyrese's wolf turned and nudged the door closed. When finished, he sat on the floor wagging his tail, much to Tyrese's disgust. This was the first time in years he'd had no control over his animal. That someone else, someone he didn't know, had control, pissed him off, and scared him.

"Come take a seat, we have much to discuss in a short amount of time. Right now your mother is enjoying the gardens, but I don't know how long she plans to stay." The man waved to a chair at the table.

Tyrese wanted to say she waited for him, but he couldn't speak. A moment later, he lay naked on the floor in human form. Because he hadn't called his wolf, the words he normally invoked to insure his clothing reappeared when he reverted to human were missing.

"There are clothes on the chair. Get dressed."

Tyrese stood and walked back to the chair. As he dressed, he glared at the man who'd just blown his theory that he and his brother could handle anything life threw at them.

"I think you know who I am, would you mind explaining who you are and what do you know of my mother?" Tyrese took a seat at the table.

"I'm Silas Knight, the Patron. This is Jayden – Alpha of this area. You and your family are guests on his pack lands and owe him thanks. I don't know how much you know or understand about Pack dynamics, but while in his territory you show him respect."

Tyrese understood and nodded. "Alpha Jayden, my thanks for the care of my family."

Jayden nodded. "La Patron promised your brother he would protect your mother and his aunt. I serve him."

Tyrese was pleased Tyrone had taken care of the women who mattered most to them. He looked at the Patron. "I owe you my gratitude." He bowed from the waist.

"It was important to do so," the Patron said, leaning back in his chair while looking at Tyrese. "Let me be clear, young wolf. I control the Alphas in this country. The well-being of the Wolf Nation is my number one priority. I have extended my protection to your family to allow me time to study the unique occurrence of your birthright."

Tyrese froze. He'd known sooner or later his father's fears would be realized. He'd hoped it would be later.

"First off, a human female gives birth to two pups. They all live healthy lives. She is not the mate of the wolf who impregnates her. There is no emotional connection to stop her from becoming impregnated again by another wolf. We have an untenable situation here. Wolves mate for life. Period. The human element upsets the balance."

For the first time since his forced change, Tyrese recognized the seriousness of the matter. "How can we explain the unexplainable?"

"You can't. Perhaps now you understand why I cannot allow the three of you to leave here until we have more answers."

Tyrese couldn't believe the nerve of the man. "What? Why? We've lived like this for years with no problems."

The older man shrugged. "Your mother has been fortunate a wolf has not taken her to bed and bred her full of pups. No one knows of her capabilities. Nor are we sure of yours. By the end of the week, your family will move to Alpha Jayden's facility for further treatment. During that time I will watch and assess you and your twin's level of competence. The two of you are the first hybrids we've come across and we need to understand more about you."

With each word, Tyrese's anger escalated, yet the men remained composed in their seats as the older one continued telling him that they were in effect his prisoners.

"No," Tyrese said, the calm tone of his voice in direct opposition to his feelings.

"Did I forget to mention the only other alternative is that I'll kill all four of you in the next few minutes if you disagree?" The words, spoken calmly made them all the more menacing.

Tyrese blew out a stream of air. "I thought you offered my mom and aunt protection, what happened to that?"

"I offered protection until your brother could retake the job himself. His test results from this morning relinquished me of that duty."

"What kinda place is this? You threaten to wipe out innocent families if they don't do what you say?" He shook his head. "Damn, the old man was right about Packs after all. They're a bunch of –"

"Watch it young wolf. You're granted a small amount of leniency because you don't understand Pack life. But if you live past today, you will learn, and learn it fast. You're speaking of things you do not know. But you do not ever disrespect the Pack, any Pack. Is that clear?"

Tyrese hesitated. A whip of power lashed across his chest, tightening until he took sips of air. "I will not ask again," Silas said in a low voice.

"I understand," Tyrese choked out. The tightness disappeared. He gasped for air, certain he'd fallen down the rabbit hole.

"Good. The first thing you need to do is convince your mother it's in everybody's best interest for her to go with her sons to therapy. All three of you must go."

"My aunt?"

"At this time she is not of interest. Based on her preference, and the fact she's had a hysterectomy, we do not fear she'll be used as a breeder."

"Breeder?" Tyrese shook his head. "How long will we stay as your guests?"

His sarcastic tone appeared lost on the Patron. "Until I am certain you pose no threat to my people."

Dread filled Tyrese. Tyrone tried to contact him through their link and he blocked him. "And my mother?"

The man shrugged. "We shall see, young wolf. I feel no real threat from her. We believe that any bitch who breeds wolves is a gift from the goddess."

Tyrese released a breath he'd been holding. "So she's safe."

"It depends on how you interpret that. One thing for sure, her activities will be curtailed for the immediate future. And you and your brother need to convince her that staying at the complex longer is a good thing. Just because we won't physically harm her, does not mean she won't suffer if she tries to run away."

Tyrese closed his eyes. His mom was going to shit bricks.

Chapter 7

TYRESE SEARCHED THE GARDENS for his mom. His heart warmed at the sight of her sitting on a bench in the middle of a patch of colorful flowers. Her emerald green short-sleeved top and jeans blended with the foliage. He paused, observing her posture. She seemed distracted. He followed her line of vision and smiled at the koi pond situated nearby. Opening his senses he inhaled, and then blunted them a bit. The smell of sickness mixed with the vibrancy of the garden had a high ick factor. He smacked his tongue to dislodge the taste.

"Mom." He watched her stiffen and then turn in his direction. For a moment he drank her in with his eyes. There was no woman on the face of the planet with a larger heart than his mom. A born nurturer, she had been the team mother for his baseball and football sports clubs. During the seasons, their home was filled with young boys vying for her cookies and cupcakes. If any of the kids needed to talk, she'd had an available ear. They'd lived so far out that life could've been boring, but she'd gone out of her way to make sure they never felt left out of the action.

"Rese?" She shaded her eyes with her hand, and then a smile lit her face. Her brown eyes glowed with love as they met halfway. He enfolded her in his arms and prayed he could keep her safe. She had no more control over the manner of her birth than he had.

"God, I missed you, Mom." He held her back a bit and looked at her. She did the same to him. "You've lost weight."

"You say that like it's a bad thing," she said as he pulled her close again.

He laughed, knowing better than to say anything else on that score. "Even if you blew up big as a house, you'd still look good to me." He placed a kiss on her forehead. "I missed you."

"I missed you too." She took his hand and led him back to the stone seat bench. "Have you talked to Rone?"

Not wanting to lie, he said. "I haven't been upstairs yet. I wanted to see you first. We can go together after you tell me what's been going on with you."

Quiet, she leaned on his shoulder. "I need to do something with my life. Maybe go to college, learn a trade. You boys are grown, have your own lives. I'm... I'm alone. I've been sitting here thinking about what I'd like to do with my life. Maybe visit Mama and her new husband in Florida, or go on a cruise." She looked up at him. "I can't remember the last time I've done something fun, something that interests me. Isn't that awful?"

The awful thing was knowing she'd be denied all of those things for her immediate future. For a few seconds, he wondered how far he'd make it if he just took her out the front door and kept walking. The memory of the Patron triggering his wolf flashed across his mind.

He was screwed.

"No, not awful." He swallowed. "Soon Rone will get a clean bill of health. Maybe you can plan to do those things after that." The words tasted like bile on his tongue.

"I don't think he wants me to come with him. Maybe I've been too clingy. Maybe it's time to back off and let you guys fly."

"Wow, you picked a sweet time to bail, Ma. I'm being released from my duties pending my psyche evaluation. And Rone's being shipped off for therapy to relearn basic skills." He shook his head, shocked to hear her sound so defeated and knowing he had to get her to change her mind.

"Ow." The sting in his forearm from her pinch cleared his head.

"Stop being a smart-ass. I'm entitled to live my life. Everybody else is," she muttered as she rubbed the spot she'd pinched.

"That's true. You've lived for us, now you should do the things that make you happy." He prayed she'd agree to do those things after Tyrone's therapy.

She patted his leg and stood.

He stood next to her.

"Let's go see your brother."

Arms wrapped around each other, Tyrese guided her through the cafeteria, aware someone watched. Good thing she talked about his aunt and didn't realize he wasn't paying much attention. After they got off the elevator and headed toward Tyrone's door, they heard a commotion. His aunt and someone else was pleading with Tyrone.

Tyrese knew the moment his mom heard what he'd picked up the moment the elevator doors had opened. His brother was out of bed, anxious to find him and his mom. He would've done the same thing.

"Rone, mom, and I just got off the elevator on your floor. Calm down." He sent the message through their link.

"What happened? Did something happen to mom?"

"No. She was in the garden looking at flowers."

"Shit!" Tyrone yelled so loud, Jasmine froze for a second and then took off down the hall, Tyrese on her heels.

"What's going on?" his mom demanded once she cleared the door.

"Your hard-headed son got it in his mind that you'd disappeared and wanted to come find you. He didn't want me to leave the room, as though he could do a better job than I could in finding you." His aunt's head snapped up, and she smiled. "Tyrese, it's so good to see you again." She walked over and wrapped him in a loving embrace.

He squeezed her tight. "It's good to see you, Aunty. You look beautiful as always." He stepped back and looked at her. She preened and did a slow turn.

"I know, but it's still good to hear."

He placed another kiss on her cheek. "Give that to Mandy for me and tell her I said hi."

"Thanks, will do. You just got here?"

"I've been downstairs with Mom in the gardens. I called earlier, and she told me she was chillin down there. I had to go see my favorite lady first."

His aunt patted his cheek even as her eyes slid to his mom. "That's good, sweetie."

"Does the doctor know you're out of bed?" Jasmine asked Tyrone.

"He does now. The nurses came and left. Why didn't you let me know where you were going? You just walked out. I thought you went to the bathroom or to grab a bite to eat. You left over thirty minutes ago." His tone went from happy to see her to accusing.

Tyrese started to interfere to save his brother from a tongue lashing but figured his mom would be in a better frame of mind after she got a few things off her chest.

"Excuse me?" Jasmine asked Tyrone in her who-are-you-talking-to voice.

He blinked, looked at Tyrese, his aunt, and then back at his mom. "I... I worried when I didn't know where you were. We don't know anyone here, so I... I wished you would'a told me you were in the gardens." His entire demeanor wilted beneath their mother's glare. She was a dollar's change away from laying into Tyrone, and Tyrese didn't think being in a public place was going to save him.

"Jazz," Aunt Renee said, looking at her watch.

His mom looked at her sister but didn't say anything.

"I've got a flight to catch, I was telling you this morning something happened. Mandy called me after I left the hotel or I would've told you then. She has me booked on the two o'clock flight. With security and everything, I need to go." While she'd been talking, she'd walked over to his mom. Now they stood face to face.

"Okay, Nay. Thanks for coming out here with me and staying. I don't know what I'd do without you." The two women embraced. Jasmine placed a kiss on her sister's cheek.

Aunt Renee cupped her sister's cheek. "Don't think I've forgotten that conversation we started before the call."

"I know you haven't. Neither have I. You may be right. After things settle here, I'd like for us to make plans."

"Thank you, Jesus. I was so scared you'd fight me on this." Renee pulled back. "Look at them." She pointed to Tyrone and him. "You've done an amazing job raising two grown men. It's time for you to think about yourself. That's what they want for you." She looked at him and then Tyrone. "Right boys? You want your mom to be happy."

"Yes, always," he said.

"Of course, she deserves it," Tyrone said as he reclaimed his bed.

His aunt clapped her hands as though she'd accomplished a tremendous feat. "Great, it's settled. Once you leave this therapy thing, we're going to set things in motion. Who knows, maybe you'll meet a handsome man, have a little fun, get laid."

"Aunty," Tyrese said, placing his hands over his ears.

"Oh lord," groaned Tyrone.

"Maybe," Jasmine said, smiling. "Take care, Renee, call me when you get home. Tell Mandy thanks for covering for you, I owe her one."

"That's how family rolls. We look out for one another." She placed a kiss on Tyrese's and then on Tyrone's cheek. "Be good boys, don't have my sister go off on you in this fancy place. You know she will."

"We know," Tyrese said. "I remember too many shopping trips when she'd go into autocorrect mode."

"God, that was embarrassing," Tyrone muttered.

Jasmine laughed. "Sometimes correction needs to take place right where you are so you never forget how to act in that place."

Tyrese leaned forward and kissed his mom's cheek. "You told us that all the time."

She shook her head. "I told you that when I had to correct your behavior in public. Think about it, how long did it take for you to remember not to open food in grocery stores or add things to my cart, or take something without paying for it?" She eyed him and his brother with a twinkle in her eyes.

"I'm sure it didn't take long. Sorry, I've got to go, but I do." Renee grabbed Jasmine's arm and walked her to the door.

If they weren't wolves, neither he nor his brother would've heard his aunt's whisper. "Wow, sis, that tall one with the green eyes might be a good place to start. As far as men go, he wasn't half bad."

"Uh, no. I'd like someone, not like Davian, thank you. And he has hard ass written all over him. The next man I take on will see me as a person first."

Tyrese looked at Tyrone and spoke through their link. *"This is not good. We have to convince Mom to go to therapy. We have to stay until the Patron is convinced we're not a threat."*

Tyrone's eyes widened. *"What?"*

Tyrese glanced at door. His mom was listening to his aunt talk about Mandy. He took a seat next to the bed. *"Yeah, I had a forced meeting with the Patron and the Alpha who runs this territory. He has concerns over her breeding wolves and not being mated."*

"You agreed?" It was weird hearing Tyrone's outrage through their link.

"It was that or we all die, including Aunty."

Tyrone's eyes widened and then closed tight. *"I did this. I brought her to their attention."*

"No. Well, maybe. But they had no idea half-breeds existed. Plus we're not rabid, or crazy. I get the idea they plan to run all types of tests on us."

"On Mom?" Tyrone sounded horrified.

"I don't think so. Not at first anyway. I do think they plan to look into her background if they haven't already."

"You believe him? You believe he'd kill us."

Tyrese thought of the power that'd pulsed in the room with little effort on the Patron's part. *"He called my wolf. One minute I was standing in the hall, the next I was on all fours prancing up the stairs like a punk answering his call. My damn wolf sat there wagging his tail like a bitch waiting for a treat."* That still rankled. His gaze swung to his twin. *"Do I believe he'd take us out? In a fucking heartbeat. In his mind, we're freaks. Something that shouldn't exist. Could be the real reason he's allowing us to live is he thinks there may be others. By understanding us, it gives him an advantage. He can prepare to deal with any others."*

"*Damn,*" Tyrone glanced at the door. His mom and aunt were hugging again. *"What's the deal with the military?"*

"I'm out, pending my psych eval. You?"

"I think I'm being discharged as well. Can't help but wonder how much clout Silas has, huh?"

Tyrese frowned, the name sounded familiar but he couldn't place it. *"Silas?"*

Tyrone nodded. *"Silas Knight, the Patron, leader of the Alpha werewolves."*

Jasmine walked over to the bed and pulled up a chair next to Tyrese. "Okay guys, what's our next move?"

Tyrese looked at her. "I think we're going to the physical therapy facility with the hard head over here who got hurt." He watched her through lowered lids, hoping she'd just fall in line with their plans. He should've known better.

She frowned and sat back. "I'm not comfortable staying out there. Can we get a place nearby?"

"I'll ask, but I thought you planned to stay with me until I recovered," Tyrone said, looking confused.

She shrugged. "I'll just be in a nearby hotel like I am now. I can visit you. But I can also see and do other things."

Tyrese grew uneasy at her bid to push them out of the nest so she could begin her journey. Although she deserved it, her timing sucked. "Mom, why can't we all stay together? This may be the last time you live with your sons, if you want to look at it like that. But I want you with me if I have to stay in a place with him." He pointed at Tyrone, who appeared offended.

"I don't want to stay in a place with just you either," Tyrone snapped.

"Can we all stay at the hotel?"

Tyrese hated to kill the hopeful tone in her voice. But he wanted her alive, to have a chance at happiness later. He banked on that being a real possibility after the Patron realized they weren't a threat.

"I can't. Sorry, Mom," Tyrone said with just the right amount of sadness.

"Oh well," his mom said with obvious false cheer. "I suppose I can put down my apprehension over this decision, just this once. But I've gotta tell you, I don't feel good about this move. Not at all." She eyed Tyrone. "Would you like to get a second opinion? You don't have to do this if you aren't sure."

It was a good thing she had no idea they were smack dab in the middle of a shifter hospital; and from what Tyrese had smelled, she and his aunt were the only humans. The man who controlled all these people made a mockery of his mom's claim. They had to do this if they wanted to live.

Chapter 8

THE THREE BEDROOM CONDO was on the second floor, situated near the wooded area of a large complex. It suited their needs. Each bedroom had a bath, and the stocked large kitchen had all types of meats and veggies. Once they arrived, after unpacking, Jasmine slept for twenty hours straight.

Tyrese's dismissal from the military, due to the strange bond with his brother, came first. It looked as though Tyrone would receive a similar dismissal. She should've been happy, but their sadness permeated their temporary living quarters and stopped her from saying anything glib.

The first five days flew by. Both boys left in the morning to do whatever they did in therapy while she stayed at the house, alone and depressed over her life. All of that came to a screeching halt on the sixth day.

She decided to go for a walk. Taking her phone, MP3 player, and headphones, she walked down the path that started near their condo building. Within minutes, the fresh air and the beauty of the flowers and nature eased her frustration about her stunted life.

When her legs began to ache, she sat on the grass near the path to rest. The sky was clear and the warmth of the sun caressed her cheek. She thought to lie down and take a rest. But the possibility of bugs crawling over her nixed that idea. After a few minutes, there was a sound somewhere behind her. She stilled, ready to run if necessary. Palming her cell phone, she listened harder. The noise sounded more like a moan this time.

She leaned forward and strained her neck to hear better.

"Owww," the sound came again, clearer this time. It sounded like a child, a wounded child.

Heart pounding, she jumped up and searched through the bushes. "Hello!" She called to let the child know she was on her way to him or her.

The moan came again, louder.

Jasmine took off running, doing her best to keep the leaves and branches from hitting her face. A few moments later she came upon the most incredible sight. A young boy lay on the ground with an animal skin blanket covering his legs and thighs. His pupils dilated, and he shook as though he was freezing, although sweat dripped from his body. The sight triggered an old memory, but as soon as she thought about it, it fled.

"Ooooo," the child moaned again.

Without thinking, Jasmine sat, took his head, placed it in her lap, and stroked him. "It's going to be okay, sweetie. Just calm down and tell me who I should call to come get you."

The child shook so hard, his lower body contorted and then spasmed. She continued whispering soothing words and stroking his head.

"Should I call 911?" She asked, more to herself than him. When he continued shaking, she dialed Tyrese.

"Mom?" He sounded out of breath.

"Rese?"

"Yeah."

"Listen, I went for a walk and found this young boy lying in the forest. I'm not sure what happened to him, but he's covered in fur and shaking. Who should I contact?"

"Where are you?"

"I just told you, in the woods off the trail. Forget it, I'll call emergency, he's shaking real bad. I hope he wasn't bit by something and having a bad reaction." She looked around for bugs or worse, snakes. Her hand squeezed the phone as she realized the possibility of being bitten.

"You need to walk out of there just in case whatever bit him comes back."

Fear choked her, but she couldn't do what her son suggested. "I'm not going to leave him alone, something is very wrong with him. He could get worse."

"I hear that stubborn note in your voice. I'll call the administrator and we'll come take care of it. You sure you're okay?"

"I've had years of experience calming boys who've had accidents, although this one is weird. His legs... anyway, get him help fast." She clicked off and continued stroking the wet strands on top of the boy's head. His breathing slowed, and he grew calmer each second.

"Help is on the way, you'll be fine," she told him.

His head moved in her lap and he looked up at her with dark brown eyes. "Thank you. What's your name?"

She smiled. "Tell me yours first."

"Callum."

"Okay Callum, I'm Jasmine. How are you feeling?"

He closed his eyes and then opened them. "Bad, but not like at first. I don't think I'm dying anymore. Thanks for that."

Surprised, she stared at him for a second and then smiled. Something inside clicked, and she shook her head as a feeling of well-being flowed through her. She missed caring for her sons like this. There was no question, when you helped others, it came back to you. But this was different, his gratitude touched a chord in her that she hadn't felt in years. It was an indefinable something that banished the darkness of her depression and filled her with light. At that moment she wanted to sing, to dance with joy, and not for any particular reason other than it was a bright day.

"Who are your parents? Should I call them?"

He lifted his head and then returned it to her lap. "He knows and is on his way."

True enough, a few moments later the quiet ceased with the arrival of Tyrone, Tyrese, Silas, and Jayden.

"Mom, stay still," Tyrese said, standing nearby.

"What?" She looked at him with a tilt of her head.

"Just stay still while his father takes him."

"Callum?"

He looked up at her with warm eyes. "That rude young man who didn't ask how you're doing is my son, Tyrese. The one standing next to him is my other son, Tyrone. They're twins. Please forgive their manners. You're the one in pain, not me."

He chuckled and then grimaced. "It's okay. Thanks for stabilizing me." He looked over her shoulder. "Dad?"

The man she knew as Jayden stepped behind her. "I need you to move so I can work on him."

"Oh, I'm sorry. I just didn't like seeing his head on the ground. Can you hold him?" She slid Callum's head to his father and slid from beneath him. When she stood, Jayden's head whipped around to stare at her.

Tyrone and Tyrese stepped closer to each side as she brushed the debris from her pants. Jayden's eyes narrowed, and he inhaled.

"Your son is in pain, if you can help him, please do it," she said, pointing at the young boy.

Jayden's forehead touched his son's forehead. A moment later the fur disappeared and a long-limbed teenager lay shivering on the ground.

"Give him your jacket, Tyrone," she demanded. When he removed it, she handed it to Callum. "Wear this."

"Yes, Ma'am." Jayden helped him put on the light-weight coat that reached his mid-thigh. He stood on shaky legs with help from his father. Once standing, he looked at Jasmine and smiled. "Thank you, I owe you my life."

Surprised, her mouth dropped. Once she processed his words, she gave him a few of her own. "Your life is yours to live. If you treat others with the same kindness I showed you, then the debt is repaid tenfold."

He paused and then nodded.

Jayden looked at her, and then at Silas. They nodded and the four of them returned to the condo. Silas accompanied them. He'd been a frequent visitor since their arrival. After placing her MP3 player and cell phone on the table, she turned to look at the three silent men.

"What just happened?"

"Huh?" Tyrone asked without looking at her.

"Don't 'huh' me? You were there. That boy's legs were furry. At first, I thought it was a blanket, but it wasn't. His furry legs were bent funny, too." Her voice hardened. "Start talking. Start by telling me how you were able to find me in the woods when I didn't give you directions. Then explain why you told me not to move. Bring it up to the child losing his furry legs and walking away when he thought he was dying." She eyed Tyrone and Tyrese. "Don't bother lying to me, either. I think there's been quite enough of that." She looked at Silas, who stood near an open window. His silhouette reminded her of Renee's comment a few days ago.

Her stomach clenched. A throbbing beat in her core.

The man flinched.

She dragged her attention back to her sons, crossed her arms, and tapped her feet. "Start at the beginning."

Two hours later, heart in her throat, tears running down her face, she stood. "You've been like this all this time and never told me?" She couldn't believe they'd done that. "All those times I worried, it was for nothing?"

"Ma, we couldn't—"

Heartbroken, she sniffed. "That's right, you couldn't tell me because of the promise you made to the man you hardly ever saw. The asshole who missed every minor and major event in your lives. The same one who spent time with you when it was convenient for him. I understand your loyalty to that person instead of me." She shrugged. Her heart shattered at the staggering amount of lies and deception. She'd given up so much and to have them keep such a critical part of them locked away seemed like treason of the highest order.

"It's wasn't like that, we thought... we thought it'd freak you out having animals for sons," Tyrone said.

Her brow dipped as she looked at him. "Unlike now, is that what you mean? Is this the face of a freaked out woman, or a woman who feels betrayed once again by those closest to her?"

"Ma, no." Tyrese walked over, dropped to his knees, and wrapped his arms around her waist. "I'm sorry. You're right, we should have told you from the beginning. But he made it seem like... it doesn't matter. I should've told you anyway. Please forgive me."

A bitter coldness filled her chest. Her family had taken so much from her. Or she'd given too much, either way, a quiet numbness filled her body. She glanced at Silas, who'd remained silent through the telling.

"Can I leave this place?" she asked him.

"No, not yet. Maybe soon." His voice remained neutral.

She nodded, knowing she should be angry, sad, disappointed, or another emotion. Yet, there was nothing. With a gentle push, she moved Tyrese, stood, and walked to her room.

Silas breathed easier once Jasmine left the room. Her pheromones were off the charts and he'd had a hard time controlling his wolf. Even Jayden had sensed it and he had a mate. Silas read the surprise and fear in the Alpha's eyes when she'd stood from holding Callum. He doubted her sons recognized the mating scent, but they'd reacted to the Alpha's response and stepped beside her.

"She's hurt," Tyrese said in a hoarse voice.

Tyrone sat in the chair with his head in his hands. "She put us in the same category as my old man. I never wanted her to see me when she thought of him. Lord, I fucked up. I can't believe I hurt her like that."

"We both did."

"No, you wanted to tell her. I convinced you dad was right. If I hadn't... I've never seen her look so... so broken. I never want to see that look again."

"I know. That's the first time she didn't accept an apology." Tyrese inhaled and blinked fast. "What if it's too much? Not the wolf thing, but she's hurt because of the lies. The years of lying about where we were and what we were doing." He covered his eyes and breathed hard.

"I don't know what to do."

Silas closed the window now that her fragrance dissipated. "Let her sleep. Tomorrow, or whenever she's ready to talk, talk. But don't push things. She has to deal with this and you in her own way."

Tyrone nodded.

"I know. There's not much else we can do," Tyrese said as he stood.

"There's another problem," Silas said.

Both of them looked at him.

"Another?" Tyrone asked with a bit of skepticism.

"But we're not done with this one yet," Tyrese said.

Silas had grown fond of the twins. They both possessed Alpha qualities and had taken to the training and studies with ease. Their honesty and how well they meshed with Jayden's Pack impressed him. That brought him back to their new challenge. He sat on the sofa next to Tyrone and spoke through their link. *"Something happened while your mom was helping Callum through his first change."*

"That was awesome, wasn't it? I thought I'd be fighting a changeling, but she treated him like a normal kid," Tyrone said.

"What do you mean, something happened to her?" Tyrese asked, meeting Silas's eyes.

"She's releasing serious pheromones." When the twins still looked clueless, he continued. *"It's a mating call. Even Jayden picked up on it and he's mated."*

Tyrese dropped his head into his hands.

Tyrone's mouth dropped open. *"My mom? What're you saying?"*

Silas pinched the bridge of his nose. *"She is releasing a scent that will call wolves to her in droves. I cannot explain why or what brought this on. She's human and this shouldn't happen."*

"What do you mean her scent will call wolves? I didn't pick up anything," Tyrone said, frowning.

"That's a good thing, asshole. She's our mother," Tyrese snapped

as he stood, placed his hands on the top of his head. *"What about the bitches? How will they deal with this... this threat to their mates?"*

"Oh shit!" Tyrone spoke aloud as it dawned on him.

"They'll kill her," Silas said without blinking. "For a mated male to be affected by another, it tears at the fabric of who we are. Mates do not share, period."

"This is not her fault. She was born like this and I guarantee she's not doing anything on purpose." Tyrese looked panicked.

Silas sighed. This situation had all types of complications he'd rather not be involved with. He looked at the scared young wolves and knew, in the end, he'd get involved. He wanted to curse to the heavens. "I know and understand. We have to keep her locked in this unit and continue our search for answers. I think a trip to Oklahoma to meet your father's Pack is in order."

"You promised we could go with you when you did that," Tyrone reminded him.

He nodded. "I know, but you can't leave, and we need answers."

"This mating thing, what do you mean? My father had a mate, but I don't think it's the same thing," Tyrese asked.

Tyrone nodded. "Good point, Rese. How does she get over this?"

"Sex. The mating call puts out an all-points bulletin that she wants to be fucked hard and heavy. And the first time she steps out that door, they'll answer her call. Their wolves will drive them to respond and it won't matter that she's human."

"They could kill her." Tyrone's eyes widened with fear.

"Yes."

Tyrese eyed him. "Is it because you're the Patron that your beast isn't driving you to do something?"

Silas chuckled without humor. "No. I stayed by an opened window to keep my beast calm. Otherwise..." he shrugged. "Take it from me, her call is strong. I have never experienced anything like it. Right now, I don't know how to keep her safe."

"Can you ward the doors so no one can enter?" Tyrese asked.

"Yes. But then no one could leave either. How will that work? And for how long?"

"I think we should tell her," Tyrese said. "She should be aware of the danger and be a part of the solution. I am not down with doing anything that involves her ever again without her knowledge."

Tyrone nodded. "When should we tell her? Does she have at least through the night?"

Silas inhaled. The scent had dimmed but his wolf was still on alert searching for the tantalizing aroma. "It's better, but she's not stirring or anything." He ran fingers through his hair. "I don't have answers for you." He looked at the two men he'd grown to respect. "We'll think of something."

Chapter 9

THE NEXT MORNING, JASMINE ROLLED over and decided not to get out of bed. With a lazy sprawl, she inhaled. The smell of bacon teased her nostrils.

"Now they cook," she grumbled and covered her head with a pillow. Her ex-husband had been a wolf or dual-natured shifter as they called themselves. Her sons were wolves. It still boggled her mind, and she'd made them prove it. They'd changed right before her eyes into huge animals.

Even then she saw Tyrese and Tyrone through the sad eyes of the beasts they'd become. Her sons, she'd given birth to them, breast-fed them, changed their diapers, and loved them unconditionally. Nothing had changed other than her feelings hurt because they'd kept her out of the loop.

A knock hit her door. "Mama?"

"Hmmm?"

"Breakfast. You want it in there?"

"No."

There were muffled sounds on the other side of the door.

She smiled, crossed her legs, and placed her arms beneath her head.

"Uh, no, you don't want your breakfast in your room, or no, you don't want anything to eat?"

She wasn't hungry, but they were trying so hard to make amends. "I'll eat at the table."

"Oh... okay. I'll put your plate on the table, then." She chuckled at the disappointment in Tyrese's voice. Apparently, they'd been hoping she'd let them in her room like she did when they were younger and wanted to apologize. Nope. They were now adults and had made that argument one time too many. Swinging her legs over the side of the bed, she stretched and headed for the shower. They could wait a little longer.

Ten minutes later she walked into the living area. Her sons jumped up and met her as she walked to the table.

"Morning, Mom."

"Morning." She sat without looking at them.

Tyrone placed a warm plate with cinnamon raisin toast, bacon, eggs, and hash browns in front of her.

She bit the inside of her lip to keep from smiling. They were pulling out all the stops. Hungry, she took a bite of toast and a sip of orange juice. The only sound in the room came from her.

Intent on eating her meal, she ignored Tyrese as he sat across from her. "Good?"

"Yes, thank you."

He frowned.

Tyrone took the other seat at the table. "Do you want us to move out?"

The fork froze. Curious, she looked at him. She hadn't thought about that, but maybe it was time. "Do they have more rooms?"

Tyrone bit his lip and turned away, but not before she read the pain in his eyes. She placed the fork on the table.

"Mom, I... we are sorry for not telling you everything, it was wrong. But please don't shut us out of your life. Not that." Tyrese took her hand. His eyes filled as he tightened his hold. "I can't lose you. Tell me how to make this right, how can I make it up to you?"

It was time to set a few things straight. It pissed her off that she wouldn't be able to hold onto her anger any longer. They'd been wrong, but she couldn't allow them to suffer like this.

"We don't live together. We haven't in over a year. That's the reason I asked. As far as what you did... it hurt. I mean it hurt buckets knowing I've been a part of your lives and didn't know my own kids." She shook her head, allowing the pain to pass through this time. "I still can't believe how you pulled it off, but you did. I guess if I hadn't stumbled across Callum, I still wouldn't know."

"The penalty for telling humans is death, Mom. Not just for the wolf, but the human as well. We couldn't risk you like that," Tyrone said his voice low and filled with sorrow.

"Last night, you didn't mention that." She searched his face for the truth, and the fact that she now felt the need to do that, hurt.

He looked surprised. "I didn't? Sorry. But that's the first thing dad taught us. Never let the humans discover who we are."

She grimaced. "Yeah, that's me. Just a human." No matter how true that designation proved to be, she despised it for becoming a dividing line between her and her sons.

"Mom."

"It's not like that."

Her head snapped up to look at Tyrone and then Tyrese. They looked away as she spoke. "It's exactly like that. And it always will be."

The quiet filled the room until Tyrese stood, took her plate, and placed it in the sink. "If you want us to move out, if that'll make you happy, we will. I don't want to, but I want you happy."

Tyrone picked up her hand. "Be mad at me, but I'm not leaving. Not now. There's time later on for us to be separated again, but not now."

"You're a brat."

His lips curved into a smile. "True, but I'm your brat."

"For now. One day you boys will have kids and I'm going to remember this day." She rubbed her hands together.

"It'll be a while, so don't get too excited," Tyrese said as he retook his seat and her hand. "I love you, Mom. I don't ever want to see you look like you did last night. Whatever it takes to make you happy, I'm on board."

"Me too." Tyrone kissed the back of her hand.

"I love you both. You know that and figured I wouldn't kill you because of that. Don't get it twisted. I'm hurt and angry. In my mind, you chose him over me and nothing you say will change that. But because I love you no matter what, I'll allow you, boys, to stay here until Jayden finds me a smaller place of my own or I leave, whichever comes first."

"Why?"

"Why?" She paused, marshaling her thoughts. "Because it's time for me to do things I've always wanted. School or art classes. I've been putting things off for years. But the last few months I've been thinking about it more and more. I'm the only person who can make lasting changes in my life. Now that I know you have a group of people who'll watch your backs, it's a good time to make changes of my own, that's all." She paused, frowning. "How much longer do we have to stay here?" She looked at Tyrone and then Tyrese.

"I'm not sure. Silas and his team are researching your background, and Dad's. They're trying to understand how you were able to get pregnant. It doesn't happen, since he's... you know."

She nodded. Uneasiness swamped her. "There's more to this than what you told me last night, isn't it?"

"Yes. Humans and wolves don't mate. They don't have kids together. It goes against everything wolves know and it's worse because Rese and I are healthy, strong potential Alpha wolves. Not weak or insane. They'd never heard of half-breeds surviving, not growing up healthy as we did. They're not sure if it was our environment or dad's genes or a combination. But it's different and they have to study those differences to decide how it'll impact their way of life."

She nodded. "Why didn't they just kill us?"

"Silas thought about it, they would have if we hadn't agreed to come here for testing and observation."

"What?" She snapped. "I was kidding." She looked from one to the other, neither smiled.

"Sorry." Tyrone looked across the room.

"Are we in danger?" She hadn't felt threatened, but then she didn't realize she was living in a place with wolves either.

Tyrese pulled his earlobe and looked at her. "No, but there's a small problem."

Her stomach dropped. Whatever it was, it wasn't small. Tyrese never got nervous. But when he did, he pulled his earlobe. "What is it and don't lie to me, never again. Don't lie, just tell me straight."

He coughed, glanced at Tyrone, and then back at her. "Did something happen yesterday while you were saving Callum?"

"What?" She couldn't follow the change in conversation.

"Yesterday... did you feel different? Strange? Did something happen while you were with him?"

"I... I'm not sure I understand what you mean by feeling different." She struggled, trying to remember. "He was moaning and in pain. I felt bad for him. It reminded me of when you boys got hurt." She shrugged. "What? Why'd you ask me that?"

There was a knock on the door. Tyrone jumped up so fast, she blinked. She craned her neck to see who was at the door.

"Morning." The deep timbre of Silas's voice touched her in places she'd forgotten existed. A tremor slid through her and settled in her core. Closing her eyes, she bit down on her lower lip as heat pooled between her legs along with a pulsating ache.

"Mom... mom," Tyrese called as he shook her.

A low growl filled the room, pulling her from her side journey. As though in a fog, she looked across the room and blinked.

Tyrone and Tyrese had pressed Silas against the window.

She stood.

"Sit."

Affronted, she placed her hands on her hips and gave him her what-did-you-say look. "Excuse you?"

"Mom, please can you sit back down? Please?" Tyrese begged while standing in front of Silas.

Shocked and concerned, she sat and crossed her arms over her legs.

"Thanks," he said, sounding more relieved than the situation warranted. After a few moments of listening to deep and heavy breathing, she peeked at the window. Tyrone was bent over, resting his hands on his knees. Silas's hands braced against the window frame, his nose pressed next to the screen. Tyrese stood in front of the other two, breathing hard as though he'd run a marathon.

"What's going on?" she asked, confused by their actions. "Did I miss something?"

Tyrese waved at his brother. "Stay here." Tyrone nodded as Tyrese walked to the table and sat. "The conversation we were having before Silas came in, remember?"

She nodded.

"You'd asked what else was going on, I was trying to understand what happened yesterday."

She frowned, trying to follow him. "Yesterday?"

"Yeah." He rubbed his neck and licked his lips a few times.

"Just tell me, Rese." Her nerves couldn't take much more of his hemming and hawing.

"You are throwing off what the other wolves consider a mating scent. Something must have triggered it yesterday. I'm—"

Her hand flew up to the base of her throat. "A what?"

He took a deep breath and then released it in slow degrees. "A mating scent. Pheromones or something like that, and it's like a red flag."

She shook her head. "A red flag? That doesn't make sense."

"Mom," Tyrese said, his voice wobbled, and then he straightened in the chair. "Your body is throwing off a scent or signal to the wolves that you want to have sex."

Her hands flew up to her mouth as her eyes widened.

"They smell it and it drives them crazy with lust. Rone and I don't, but Silas did when he walked inside."

"Oh my God." She covered her face remembering her lust-filled thoughts a minute ago. A thought hit her. "Wait, what does this mean?" She paused, her eyes narrowed. "Is this why you and Rone are still here? The reason you've been here all morning?"

"Part of it. We couldn't leave knowing you were mad at us anyway. We planned to talk to you about this and discuss the best way to handle it."

"Handle it?" She didn't understand what they expected her to do. She couldn't control her thoughts.

"Silas, is there a way to stop this?" Tyrone asked the man standing behind him.

"It'll stop when she's no longer in need."

"Damn," Tyrese said.

"Watch your mouth," she said automatically while thinking over Silas's comments. "In need? Is that what this is about?"

"Mom…"

"Shush, Tyrese. I'm talking to Silas."

"I believe so. You have to understand, we don't know how things work with you. We are blind in a lot of ways. But when our bitches are in heat, a hard fucking session would clear up the situation."

"Hey, watch it. You're talking to my mom," Tyrese said, standing, jaw clenched.

"Correct, she asked me a question, and I answered her, not you, Pup. Today is not the day to try me. I am walking on the edge here. Wolves are circling below, should I leave and let you deal with them?"

"Tyrese stay out of it. Mom and Silas are talking." Tyrone crossed his arms over his chest and looked out the window.

"The fact that I was thinking of having sex has got you like this?" She couldn't believe that was all it was to it. "If that's the case how do you guys get anything done?"

"Are you ovulating as well?" Silas asked, his face turned to the window.

"I don't know. Does it matter?"

"Yes. Your body is primed and ripe during that time. But this feels different, I'm not sure why, but it's stronger, more potent. Even my wolf is not immune, and that is rare." The bite in his voice spoke of his displeasure of the situation.

"Okay, so if I have sex…"

"Ugh," Tyrese groaned.

"Stop it son. I'm trying to solve a serious problem. I don't want to get hurt and I don't want you boys hurt either. So unless you have something positive to add to the conversation, keep quiet."

He nodded but turned in his chair.

"So having sex will fix this?"

Silas inhaled and then released it. "I don't know. Perhaps. That's what happens with our females. You... you seem unaffected, that's not the case with bitches. They ache and need fulfillment in the worse way."

His words conjured up images that struck at her core. She bent forward.

"Damn it, Silas. Stop talking." Tyrese grabbed her around her waist and drug her into her bedroom.

"Please, calm down, Silas. I can tell your wolf is close to the surface. It's because she's responding to you, isn't it?" Tyrone asked nervously.

Silas tried to speak around the teeth crowding his mouth. He'd never lost control like this and he didn't like it, not one bit. She was human for shit's sake.

"That may have something to do with it," Silas growled. The little tease wanted him, and his wolf responded to her siren call. He didn't want added complications by linking himself to her.

"Silas, I don't want to lose my mom. When you first got here there were two wolves downstairs, now there's more than ten. No way Rese and I can hold off all of them. Please, tell me how to fix this. She wouldn't be in this mess if it weren't for me."

Silas understood the misplaced guilt on the young wolf's shoulder. And he knew they'd die to protect their mother. But it wasn't that simple. "Get your brother out here, but leave your mom in her room. I can breathe and think better with her in there."

Tyrone nodded and sent his brother a message through their link. A minute or two passed before the bedroom door opened and Tyrese came forward.

He stopped a few feet from them, crossed his arms, and braced his legs apart. "Yeah?"

"Silas wants to talk to us and we should hear him out."

Tyrese nodded. Something loosened in Silas's chest. He didn't want to destroy either of these young wolves, but they had to agree to stand back if they didn't want their mother to be raped by one of the circling wolves.

"Your mother wants me. That's the reason her pheromones spiked when I entered the room. Once we opened the window her scent hit the compound and now there's a collection of randy wolves downstairs. Jayden is trying to contain them and I have warded the door." He pointed to the entrance. "We cannot punish the wolves for being themselves anymore than we'd punish your mother for her desires." He paused, watching Tyrese's fist open and close.

"I can take her, drain off her energy."

"Take her?" Tyrese asked, his eyes narrowing.

"What word would make it easier for you?" Silas snapped, growing frustrated. Despite what his wolf wanted, he wasn't too keen on lying with a human. He didn't speak to them, let alone touch them.

Tyrese turned away.

"Is this the best solution?" Tyrone asked, his brow furrowed trying to work through this complicated problem.

Silas resisted the urge to run his hand through his hair. "Like I told your mom, I don't know. This shouldn't be happening at all. I don't understand why she's affecting our wolves in this manner."

Tyrese turned, stuffed his hands in his pockets, and looked at Silas. "Would you talk with her, explain everything and give her a choice? I can't do it. This ... this is my mom and I can't, don't, see her the same way you do. Maybe, Rone is right and we need to step back and let the two of you work things out." His lips twisted in a rueful expression. "You may be right in your assessment; she didn't seem upset at the idea of the two of you."

Silas appreciated the level of trust from the young wolves and their ability to think along rational lines amid conflict. They'd make fine

Alphas one day. He nodded and walked to the door. Before opening it, he looked back at them. "It might be better if she doesn't know you're out here, listening, if you get my drift."

The twins' faces dropped and they all but ran to their rooms.

He chuckled.

Chapter 10

THE SCENT OF HER NEED gut-punched him as he walked through the door. It was all he could do to stay upright.

"Jasmine?" he ground out.

She stuck her head out from behind the bathroom door. Her skin glistened in the dimness of the room. "Silas? What... what are you doing in here?" She grabbed a peach-colored robe and covered her nakedness as she looked at him.

He closed his eyes to gain control of his beast. "Stay there. Please, be still." It took a few moments, but soon he could open his eyes. He refused to look at her, no need to tempt his wolf. "Your sons thought we should continue our conversation without them. It is too difficult for them to listen."

"I see."

He didn't think she did, but they needed to bring this thing to a head. Information of a similar situation in Mexico arrived this morning, and he intended to head southwest to investigate. His Alphas near Texas knew of his imminent arrival, but he couldn't leave until he settled this manner.

"We need to have sex, shut down the mating call."

She leaned against the wall. "Is that right?"

He gritted his teeth as her fragrance teased him. "Yes. The sooner the better."

"Can I leave afterward?"

"No."

"When can I leave?"

"Once we understand how you're able to do the impossible and what impact it'll have on my people."

She frowned. "How long will that take?"

"As long as it takes," he growled. "Now lay your tempting ass on that bed or do you want me to come get you?"

Her head whipped around. Her mouth dropped and then snapped closed. "Tempting ass?" She grinned and drew her robe closer around her waist. "What if I don't want to have sex with you?"

"You do. Stop with the games." He pulled his shirt over his head and threw it on the chair.

Her eyes widened as they roved over his body.

He unsnapped his pants.

She licked her lips and released another round of pheromones.

A shudder wracked his large frame. He kicked off his shoes, and pulled off his pants, kicking them to the side.

She remained still, watching him as though fascinated.

"Bed." He pointed to the furniture.

She looked up, met his eyes, and licked her lips. "Come get me," she whispered.

Without another word, he reached her in three long strides, picked her up under her arms, turned, and dropped her on the bed. Her legs fell open. He feasted on the sight of her large, firm breasts, taut dusky nipples, and wide hips. This was a woman made for loving.

He placed a hand on each of her legs, widening them further. Her center was moist with fragrant juices that beckoned.

He plunged his finger into her warmth.

She squealed and tried to move backward. He held her in place with his palm.

"You can take this, it's just my finger." He pulled it out, licking her sweet pussy juice. The flavor was divine.

"Mmmm." He dipped low and his mouth followed where his fingers had just been. His tongue gave an experimental lick on her tender folds and it earned him a sharp gasp. Pleased, he continued licking her, drawing out more of her juices before he twirled his tongue on her clit.

"Sweet, tasty," he murmured as her legs quivered and clutched his head.

"Oh... oh..." She cried as he increased his oral assault. He couldn't get enough of her. The more he licked, the more she gave.

"I'm... oh my God... I can't... I'm," she babbled as she held his head in place.

"Let it happen. Let go," he murmured against her lips before flicking her clit again with his tongue. She stiffened and screamed her release. When the last of her tremors stopped, Silas moved upward and thrust his hips up in one stroke, burying half of his cock deep inside her.

She screamed.

He remained still, giving her a moment to get accustomed. He couldn't believe how tight she was.

"You could've warned me." She slapped him on the back.

"Why? You knew this was coming."

"Still, you should've said... something."

"Something." He pulled out and slammed back in, this time giving her his entire length.

Her breath hitched as she took all of him.

Impossible. Disbelief filled him to the point he looked down for verification. He filled her snug sheath. She shouldn't be able to take all of him.

She slapped his hips, squeezed her inner muscles, and bucked upward. "Giddy-up."

The tight feel of her heat wiped every other thought from his mind. He grabbed her hips tight as he pistoned himself in and out of her, faster and faster he rode between her thighs, unable to quench the fire in his gut. The need to bring her to heel, to have her submit to him in this primal way, stole his breath.

"Take it," he growled. "Take all of me."

She screamed his name as she came once more. He pulled out and exploded on her stomach. Ropes of pearly cream fell on her stomach and across her breast. It took everything within him not to rub his essence into her skin like lotion.

She wasn't his, he needed to remember that. "Let me get a towel." He stood, but it took a moment for him to regain his strength. He plucked the damp towel from the bathroom door and wiped his jizz from her stomach and breasts. She opened her legs.

He looked up at her.

She winked with a lewd grin.

His wolf took that as a challenge, but he fought to control his beast. Instead, he took the towel and placed it between her legs cleaning her with soft strokes. As he swiped the cloth against her puffy lips, she moaned.

"Mmmm…" Her hips flexed as his fingers replaced the towel. Pretty soon she writhed like a kitten, purring beneath his hand.

A frisson of awareness rolled up his back at her ability to tempt him to the degree that his wolf alternately snapped and whined to savor her again.

Throwing the towel aside, he crawled between her legs, lifted them high around his waist, positioned himself, and slid inside her hot, velvety, sheath. He paused for a second to control his animal. The exquisiteness of her tight tunnel shook him. With measured intent, he withdrew and slid inside again. He took her hard and deep, growling with pleasure.

The bed shook beneath them. The frame rocked against the wall, keeping time with his punishing pace.

"Ohhhh," she screamed amidst his grunts.

Her walls tightened. He shuddered and his thrusts quickened. He slammed into her, their thighs connected with a slap.

"Oh my God, oh my God," she wailed as her body grew taut.

He groaned as his own body strained to the point of pain, wanting to join her in the heady bliss of her sexual release.

Her body shuddered, stiffened. Strong vaginal muscles tightened and squeezed his rod.

"Arghh" he groaned as his back bowed. His release rolled up his back, tiny licks of fiery pleasure exploding every second. He pulled out as ropes of his release hit her belly.

"That was... that was incredible." She looked at him with dreamy eyes.

Silas frowned.

She should be drained and on her way to sleep. Instead, she looked alert and ready to go again. Perhaps he'd taken it easy on her since she was human, but he didn't think so. He glanced around the room until his eyes fell on the clock. They'd been at this for an hour already. Although her scent hadn't subsided, it wasn't as strong. Her body wanted more.

And that stung.

His fingers stroked the full length of her drenched sex, toying with her opening for natural lubrication. She gasped. Her legs spread further apart in invitation.

He smiled. She was a hot little thing, so wet, so hot against him. He eased one finger inside her.

She groaned and moved her hips. The scent of her arousal washed over him. He hooked the finger and exited. He reinserted it back with another finger.

"Yes... oh yes," she cried out, her hips moving in tandem with his strokes. His breath caught as her thighs tightened and shook. Human or not, she was beautiful in her passion. He continued to stroke her spot, enjoying how her body trembled and peaked beneath his hand.

A moment later she screamed as she came. His finger remained in her tight sheath as it tried, without success, to milk him dry. "Hmmm, greedy."

"Huh?" she asked from beneath him.

He looked at her for a moment, wondering if his need to ensure she didn't breed for him was the reason he hadn't given her what she needed. "I need to tell you something."

She blew out a breath and looked at him. "Okay."

"This time I'm going to come inside you."

She blinked and leaned up on her elbows. "With a condom?"

He frowned, insulted. As the Patron his seed was a gift, he never used condoms. Rather than chastise her for the unintentional insult, he spoke of human fears. "No. I have nothing you can catch."

"Then why have you decided to switch?"

"Maybe the reason your body's still hungry is that you need a full load of seed. And I've been wasting it on your stomach and other places."

She jerked. "What makes you say that?"

He shrugged, not wanting to get into her supposed frailty as a human. That last time, he'd slammed into her as hard as he'd slammed into any wolf bitch, she'd taken it and was up for an immediate finger tease.

"Let's just say it's a hunch. The only reason I didn't come inside you before is I don't want you to get pregnant."

"Pregnant?" Her brows furrowed as though she'd forgotten the mating scent.

"Yeah. We're still trying to figure out how this works. I don't want the water muddied."

"Oh." She looked up at him. "How many kids do you have?"

He paused and then answered. "None."

"Hmm..." She licked her lips. He fought back a growl. "Well, I don't know what to say."

"I've never had pups. I do not want my first litter to be half-breeds," he snapped.

Her head whipped up, eyes narrowed, she asked. "How old are you?"

The question surprised him. He answered without thinking. "A little over three hundred."

She gasped and then smirked. "Well if you were going to have pups, it should'a happened before now don't you think?"

His brows snapped together as he squeezed her thighs in his palms. "I'm going to take you from behind, fill you with my essence and if you breed, you will not be leaving here anytime soon. Not until my pups are born, are we clear on that?"

"But... I thought you didn't want kids from me." She sounded confused.

"I don't. But I'm the Patron and if the Goddess sees fit to bring life to my seed in you... then I'll deal with it."

She looked at him for a moment and pushed back. "That's not a risk I want to take, Silas. I've already gone through half-hearted parenting with my ex. If there's a chance I could get pregnant, I don't want to take it. In time I'll meet someone and if we decide to have kids, so be it. But at least my kids will know they're wanted, loved by more than their mother." She moved to stand.

His palms tightened on her thighs. "You're still releasing that damn scent."

She patted his hand as though he were a toddler. "It's better, I'll handle it."

A red mist rose before his eyes. She wanted someone else, impossible. "How do you plan to handle it when you couldn't take care of it earlier?"

She shrugged and tried to remove his fingers. "Look, I'm making major changes in my life." She frowned. "At least I was." She glanced at him with a small smile that tugged the corner of his heart. "Tonight was the first time I understood what all the fuss was about. I had my first, second, third, and tenth orgasm with you. That's never happened. Thanks for that. I'll always appreciate what we shared, but—"

"Stop with the damn speeches," He snorted. She'd forgotten the few lessons her sons had given her about wolf culture. He was more animal than man right now and his beast would never leave without finishing the damn job. Resigned to the possibility of half-human pups, he reflected that Tyrone and Tyrese weren't bad. Now to get this fiery temptation to stop uttering nonsense so they could get on with it.

"We're not finished and you know it. I am going to fuck you hard without a condom. Then I'm going to fill you with my seed, which should put you to sleep. There will be no more mating calls, damn it. This ends now." He leaned near her face. "Got that?" Her eyes narrowed. For a moment he thought she'd balk. But the curl of her lips as she returned his stare sent blood rushing to his rod.

"Yeah," she said in a low breathy tone.

"Get on your knees." He leaned back to give her room to comply, not missing the way her body shuddered when she moved.

He palmed her ass, slapped one cheek and then the other before squeezing them again. "Nice, firm." His lips brushed over the places he'd just smacked. Her soft ass wiggled as she moved. He tapped her thighs. "Open wider."

She spread her knees further apart.

He smiled at how sopping wet she was for him before he'd even touched her. "Beautiful," he whispered before he tongued her opening and lapped her juices. Their combined flavors exploded on his taste buds. His beast stirred as he held her tight and screwed her with his tongue. He couldn't seem to get enough.

Her scent grew stronger.

His beast rose to the forefront, growling, urging him to bite her, to take her. Lost in his lust, he rose and thrust into her warmth. Instead of screaming, she sighed and pushed back against him.

His beast pushed for him to take her hard. He pulled out and slammed into her again, mindless with pleasure. She was so fucking tight, so hot, and felt so good squeezing him. He grabbed her waist with both hands, holding her body still as he bucked into her. His pounding became a blur as he struggled to reach his pinnacle.

"Yes," she screamed. "More."

With those words, he lost control and couldn't hold onto his restraint any longer. He drove into her, pounding her relentlessly. Her moans set him aflame. He held her breast as he took her hard from the rear, slamming into her as her body stiffened. She screamed out his name, shattering as loud breathy moans escaped her throat.

On the brink of his release, he jerked hard into her and gave one last thrust as his world exploded in total bliss. His body shuddered and convulsed. Spurt after spurt of his semen filled her warm cavern as she tightened her muscles, milking him as though to draw the last dregs of his cream inside her.

She fell forward to the bed. "Okay, I call uncle. That should do it," she said in a hoarse whisper.

He pulled out and winced at the amount of fluid that flowed down her leg and onto the bed. Rolling to the side he lay next to her.

As much as he wished otherwise, this human had taken everything he and his wolf gave her. She was still a mystery, except now delicious as well. He couldn't remember ever being this sated. His wolf chuffed in satisfaction.

He sniffed. Her scent was changing. A smug measure of pride at meeting her needs filled him. She rolled over to face him.

"I need to take a shower and change these sheets," she whispered.

He yawned, unconcerned. "Let your sons do it. That way they'll know you're alright."

She gasped and sat straight up in the bed. "Oh my God. Tyrone and Tyrese. I forgot..." Her head swiveled from side to side as though they were in the room. "They heard." She dropped her face into her hand. "Never, and I do mean never, have they..." She threw her legs off the bed and ran into the bathroom.

Of course, her sons had heard her screams of pleasure and demands for Silas to fuck her. There was no doubt the wolves below had heard since her bedroom window was open. Idly, he wondered where she got the energy to run to the bathroom, he didn't want to move. The shower turned on and he glanced at the clock. With slow measured strides, he followed her. He had time for a quickie.

Chapter 11

SILAS AND HIS SMALL group parked outside the tall adobe walls of the Mexican wolves' compound. He'd received a report that these wolves kept human breeders and used them to swell their ranks. He'd requested a meeting with the pack leader who declined.

That was unacceptable.

So far they'd talked to three wolves before receiving correct instructions to this compound.

"Any ideas how to get inside and find the women," Tyrone asked. He and Tyrese worked on his security detail. Ever since Silas bedded their mom, things had been tense in the condo. All three of them agreed this break was necessary, and since the mating call had dissipated, Jayden assured him of his ability to keep Jasmine safe.

From what Silas could tell, Callum spent as much time with Jasmine as possible. The teen wolf idolized her.

Silas hadn't seen or spoken to Jasmine since he'd shut down her mating call. Things had been busy, and he didn't want her or her sons to think that the sex meant more than it did.

"I'll call him again and ask for another meeting." Silas was too far away to grab hold of any of the wolves behind the walls. He pulled out his cell and waited for someone to answer the phone. Once they did, he grabbed hold of the other person's wolf.

"Open the gate. Don't allow anything to stop you. Do it now."

He ignored the startled looks from the twins, Theron, his Alpha for Texas, and Buck, another wolf from the Texas pack.

No one spoke as they waited.

The blistering sun created oven-like temperatures inside their jeeps despite the air conditioning running full blast. Sweat ran down their bodies unchecked, but they remained quiet and resolute. After ten or more minutes, a side door they hadn't noticed before, opened a crack. Silas threw out a barrier in front of him to protect against surprises, stepped out, and headed for the entry.

The twins ran ahead to enter first. They sniffed the air and sent him a report through their mental connection.

"Ambush. About twenty wolves are hiding inside the walls."

"Just twenty?" Silas smiled through the link. *"They could have made it interesting."* He tapped Tyrone on the shoulder. *"Wait for my mark,"* he said through their links. Now that he was closer, Silas eyed the inner walls of the complex. There were twenty more wolves inside, making a total of forty plus or minus wolves.

But he didn't care about them, he searched for the human women. He was about to call off the attack when he sensed the first human heartbeat. It moved, downward. Was there more than one? He continued searching. There was another one, also moving. He smiled, at least the women were in the same place. Just as he was about to deal with the wolves, he sensed another human heartbeat. That made three. Except she moved upward. He wondered at that.

He opened his palm, released a breath, and then squeezed his fist, sending forth a compulsion to do his will.

The first wave of power pulsed through the yard. A cacophony of yelps and whines rose in volume. Silas opened his hand again and closed his fist slower this time, sending power outward to control the wolves. He waited for a bit and nodded to the twins.

As they strode through the courtyard, he watched as the wolves lay on their backs exposing their bellies to him. He nodded and continued unchallenged. These wolves were cannon fodder. Silas sent them into the forest with a mental push and command not to return until he called for them. No need to hurt the pups. The ones inside were a different matter. He was prepared to destroy them to get the answers he sought.

One large black wolf whined and circled him. Silas shooed the pup with another command. With a long whine, the pup ran toward the forest.

The twins stood on both sides of the door waiting for his command.

"Knock on the door."

Tyrone's brow rose, but he knocked. Footfalls came forward. A small woman opened the door. The terrified omega tried to greet them but shook too hard.

"Tell your master, La Patron is here to speak with him."

She nodded, bowed, and backed away from the door, her feet almost soundless on the hard floor. Seconds later, Tyrone did a backflip and changed mid-air, landing a few feet away as four wolves ran out the entry. Two veered toward Tyrese.

Silas stopped Theron from interfering; he'd seen the twins in action at the compound. But he wanted to see how they fought other hybrids. Frowning, Silas assumed the wolves from Pedro's pack were from the humans but wasn't sure.

Snarling, Tyrone leapt forward, backing the wolves away from Silas and Theron. He then charged the closest brown wolf, knocking it back, and then whirling on the other wolf, biting its hindquarters. The wolf fell. Tyrone jumped on the first wolf, grabbed it by the neck, and shook it. The wolf stopped fighting and lay supine beneath Tyrone's jaw. The entire time Tyrone held the wolf in his jaw, he watched the other wolf that lay heaving on its side.

Tyrese jumped up, missing the grey wolf by inches who charged him. When he dropped, he changed and swiped his paw across the neck of his challenger, the wolf rolled and lay on its side. The other wolf turned and leapt at Tyrese. With a snap of his jaw, he clamped around the wolf's throat, shook it a couple of times, and then dropped the dead wolf. The fight lasted just a few minutes, much to Silas' disgust. Those Mexican wolves had made the mistake of thinking the twins were weak links.

Silas never traveled with weak wolves.

Another wolf came out through the opened door and Tyrese growled, waiting for the wolf to clear the porch. Instead of fighting, the wolf whined. Head down, it trotted to the wolf lying on the ground and nudged its head. When the wolf didn't move, the smaller wolf sat next to it, whining.

Pleased with the fighting prowess of the young wolves, Silas commanded them to stay alert so they could do what they'd come to do. Silas released a breath as the twins howled their victories. He'd need to talk to them about the appropriateness of such gestures when they were in the middle of a take-over.

Silas understood the need to stand your ground, but when a bigger wolf knocked on your door, a certain amount of respect and courtesy should be shown. Silas had received neither.

He looked into the dim hall and pushed a powerful compulsion in his voice. "Pedro, come here." There were gasps of surprise. Yelps and whines came from inside the building. "Come here now, Pedro."

The slap of paws on tile filled the air. Seconds later, a large silver wolf stood in the doorway growling and baring teeth with hackles raised.

Silas looked at the pack leader and sighed. "Is today the day you die? So be it, but I did call first to make an appointment. All I wanted was to talk, and you ignored my demand. I have traveled far to gather information. So... you tell me, is today the day you and more of your pack dies?" He looked over his shoulder. Tyrese and Tyrone were still in wolf form standing over their kills. Silas sent a wave of power that dropped the arrogant wolf to his knees.

Eyes wild, the wolf continued to growl and snarl.

Silas shrugged and sent a message to his men. *Change back and move to the side.* The twins phased back and moved to the opposite side of the porch. The next moment the thunder of running wolves filled the air. Pedro's eyes widened as if he couldn't believe his ears. Wolves soon flew out the building to the yard and paced in front of the porch. Their eyes flicked from Pedro to Silas.

"No Alpha puts their pack at risk the way you did," Silas said before he turned to the Pack. "Beta, come forward." A whine rent the air as another large silver wolf walked as though being dragged against his will.

"You're not going to work either," Silas said, looking over the group. He didn't have time for pack politics. *"Tyrese, Tyrone,"* he spoke through their link. *"They took two women downstairs and one upstairs; find them and bring them here so I can talk to them."*

The two men stepped over Pedro and walked through the entrance.

"Show me your bellies," Silas said. All but three wolves dropped at once.

Theron, the Alpha of Texas shifted into a large silver wolf. He leapt and caught the first wolf by the neck, and turned while holding that wolf, knocking back the other two wolves who'd come at him from the rear. After breaking the neck of the first wolf, he rushed toward one of the others, separating them. He picked the smaller wolf and quickly dispatched him. That left the beta.

The wolves jumped at each other, but Theron was larger and brought the beta to the ground, and snapped at his neck. The wolf backed away before Theron had a grip. The Alpha charged again, and this time overpowered the beta, grabbed him by the neck, and snapped it. Theron pranced in front of the pack and then sat on his haunches near Silas.

Silas looked over the pack. "Is there any here to challenge Pedro for pack leadership?"

A large black wolf trotted back inside the gate. Silas remembered him as one of the wolves he'd sent to the forest.

The wolf sat on his haunches and transformed. "I'll challenge him." The man stood and braced his feet apart.

"And you are?" Silas asked, smiling at the growls from Pedro.

"Philippe."

"A relative or former friend? What are you doing here?"

"I lived here before Pedro and his bullies showed up, raping and killing our people. Bastardo cares nothing for the Pack, just his sick fantasies."

Silas glanced at Theron, instructing him to handle things. These wolves would fall under his direct authority. Theron shifted.

"What makes you qualified to take on the Pack," Theron asked as he stood. At six feet five inches tall with a barrel chest, thick muscular arms, and legs, the Alpha was one few dared challenge. Right now, his piercing gray eyes looked over the Pack of wolves as though he could see into their hearts and minds. With a quick flick of his hand, he brushed his long dark hair away from his face as he waited for a response.

"I'm not sure I am qualified, but I'm willing to fight the downward direction the Pack's headed."

Theron stared a moment longer and nodded. "Understand, you will be under my supervision and training if you survive the fight." He looked at the remaining wolves. "I am Alpha Theron, La Patron's Alpha of Texas. Whoever becomes Pack leader here today will be under my supervision. Is that understood?"

Silas released the wolves, and they all changed back to humans except Pedro. Theron asked them the question again, except this time he asked in Spanish. The wolves appeared surprised and then relieved. They began speaking at once, asking questions.

"Silence. There is a leadership challenge that must be dealt with," Theron said. He turned and addressed the challenger. "Philippe, do you challenge your pack leader, Pedro, for Pack leadership?"

"Yes, I do." He shifted into his wolf and loped forward. He dipped his head to Silas and stepped back. Theron nodded in approval and spoke to the Pack leader. "Pedro, there is a challenge to your leadership and you will answer in a fight to the death."

Silas released Pedro. He shook himself a few times, and then pranced down the steps, snarling at the Pack and his challenger. Philippe returned his snarl and waited for Pedro to make his move as they circled one another.

Pedro's pride and anger had him leaping for the wolf. Philippe sidestepped him and bit his left flank. Pedro howled and charged again. This time he connected, but Philippe fought with skill and heart drawing blood. The fight dragged on longer than Silas would've liked. The twins had the three women seated in one of the rooms and he wanted to question them. But he needed to stand beside his Alpha and make sure the change in command went without more bloodshed.

Minutes later, Philippe stood over Pedro, breathing heavy and bleeding. The wolves cheered and walked over to the two combatants.

"I'm going inside to question the women. Gather as much information about this operation as possible. I want to know if any women left this compound, who took them, and where'd they go. I have called the wolves from the forest, they return now," he told Theron.

"Yes, Sir."

"Will the Pack stay here or will you take them to Texas?"

"I'm not sure of their skill sets. Once Buck and I meet with the entire Pack I'll inform you of my decision."

"Good." Silas walked into the dim building. It was cool, well furnished, and in good condition. That'd be a plus if the pack remained. He rounded the corner, opened a door, and stepped into what appeared to be a large office. Tyrone and Tyrese stood near the exits while three human women sat on the leather sofa and chairs.

"Hello, I'm Silas Knight, how are you ladies today?" He strode forward and took a seat opposite them. Surprised by how young they were, he'd place them all in their twenties. They weren't beautiful, but not bad-looking. The woman in the chair had an air of entitlement about her and if he had to guess, he'd say she'd been the one taken upstairs. He eyed her a little longer.

Dark wavy brown hair flowed down her back. Large brown eyes in a heart-shaped face, narrow nose with an upturned tip at the end and a creamy unblemished complexion returned his examination. "I am Arianna and I am well, thank you." Her voice held a hint of Texas twang and he stiffened.

Had the wolves kidnapped an American? He nodded and decided

to get to that later. Turning to the other women, he waited for them to introduce themselves.

"I'm Leara." The petite dark-haired woman said, looking at him from beneath her lids. Although all three women appeared around the same age, the actions of the women on the sofa made them seem younger.

"I'm Leann," the other woman said. Both females on the couch sat with their heads down and their hands clasped in their laps. He sensed there'd been no abuse. They appeared healthy.

"Tell me how you got here." He looked at the woman in the chair.

The woman threw back her head and laughed, it was dark, sultry. "So it's true, you want conversation, nothing more?"

Silas leaned back in his seat, crossed one leg over his knee, and looked at her. The more he looked, the lovelier she appeared. "Yes. I want to understand how human women give birth to wolves."

"He's such a fool. He didn't believe your request was genuine, he thought you came to take us from him." She waved her hand toward the other women and then rested it on her stomach, drawing Silas's gaze.

"You are pregnant?"

She nodded. "We all are." She waved to the other women. "He gets crazy when we're in this condition." She paused and then shrugged. "Ah well. Your question. Let me think, it has been years and no one bothers to ask these things anymore."

"Years?" Silas frowned. "How long have you been like this?"

She closed her eyes, her lips moved as though she were counting sheep. "A hundred and twenty-eight years, I believe, give or take a few."

It took a lot to surprise Silas, but she'd just won the Oscar with her announcement. "Impossible," he whispered. She didn't look a day over twenty-five.

She shrugged. "Before the rape, blacks had to sit on the back of the bus. Mexico was in the midst of a civil war, and women couldn't vote. A lot has changed over the years."

Silas blinked. A chill slid down his back. "Raped? Is that what bought about this change in you?" As far as he knew, Jasmine was born this way. Her husband had been her first sexual partner and until a few days ago, her only partner.

She sighed as she pulled her legs beneath her and leaned back. "I think that was it. Married, I had two boys already. My husband was an abusive ass. I shouldn't have been out at night buying milk and food, but..." she shrugged. "Anyway, someone raped me. I went home and told him. He didn't believe me of course. He knocked me around a bit for being late and that was it."

"Did the man who raped you, bite you?" Silas wondered how the change in her body took place.

She thrust forward her arm. "You mean like this?" Healed teeth marks ran up and down her arm.

Mesmerized by the number of marks, he rose from his seat to get a better look. She pulled her top to the side. His eyes widened at the marks on her neck, shoulders, and upper arm. She'd been someone's chew toy.

Tyrone and Tyrese had stepped closer for a better look and then moved back. He heard the surprise and concern in their minds.

Silas fingered one of the more ragged scars. "Yes, did he bite you as he raped you?"

Her eyes fluttered closed and a sigh of pleasure rose from her lips. Silas returned to his seat. His wolf hadn't stirred although his cock had sprung to life at her actions. When she opened her eyes, she appeared disappointed.

"No. If he had, I might've been able to convince my husband what happened. Six or seven months later I gave birth to twin girls. They weren't my husband's."

"How can you be so sure?" Silas asked.

"I hated him and never allowed his seed to enter me. I did other things for him; as long as he reached his peak, he didn't care. The alcohol made him believe anything I told him," she said as though she discussed the weather.

"Where are your daughters?"

She shrugged. "Someone stole one when she was thirteen, and then took me soon after that. I never heard anything about my family again."

A throbbing pain built behind Silas's eyes. This whole impossible situation was worse than he'd thought. "Who stole you? Pedro?"

She laughed and shook her head. It sounded rusty as though she never used her vocal cords in that manner. "No. Pedro is one of a few. The first pack leader took me someplace cold, up north I believe." She rubbed her forehead. "It has been years. He was kind in a gruff way. I gave him many sons."

"Over the years, any idea how many girls you've birthed?" The women were the key and someone, an enemy no doubt, realized this and set them loose in his back yard.

"Other than these two?" She nodded to the women on the couch.

Uneasy, Silas nodded. He'd detected human heartbeats from those women.

She closed her eyes again, her lips moved as she counted.

Silas glanced at Tyrone and Tyrese. They stared at the woman with a frown. Today they would discover how fortunate they'd been having a loving mother, whether that special care affected the wolf-pack or not, Silas couldn't say.

"I'm going to say at least twenty. Since the rape, I've always had multiple births, always the same sex." Her eyes narrowed as she looked toward the ceiling, shaking her head. "That seems about right, nine or ten pregnancies with females over the years."

"How old were you when you changed?" He mulled over the implications. Did the women keep their human form and the male wolves turn into wolves? The idea was too over the top to voice. He half-listened while his mind processed his unspoken questions.

"Around twenty-four." The woman smiled at him and flipped her hair over her shoulders.

"So... this process keeps you from aging?"

"I guess. How old are you, Leara?" she asked, looking toward the sofa.

"I'm twenty-five."

Silas couldn't believe it. There was no record of this infraction anywhere. How had this been kept quiet for so long? His thoughts returned to the book of warfare and the biblical strategy. It fit but didn't make sense. More importantly, who was the enemy who had set this atrocity in motion?

"Let's get back on track. Someone raped you, then you had female twins. One disappeared in her teens. You don't know what happened to the other because wolves took you somewhere up north. How long did you stay there?"

She shrugged. "I don't know. The pack lived far in the mountains. When they stole me from that pack, I remember being surprised that women wore pants, smoked, and drove cars. The next pack took me down south, near the river that cuts through the country. The bitches in that pack didn't appreciate me giving birth to pups while they had to wait to find mates before they could get pregnant. They attacked me all the time. I heard they killed my pups." She shrugged, although her voice had saddened. "The fighting got old. The pack leader sent me to another pack near Mexico. Pedro stole me from there. They were my next litter." She tipped her head to the women on the sofa. "I have been here since then."

"You fought wolf bitches?" Tyrone asked.

She shrugged. "Yeah. It was a surprise. I'm no wolf, can't change or anything. But I heal faster than a wolf. I'm fast and strong. Surprised the shit out of everyone the first time I knocked a bitch out. Stopped them from picking on me so much, until they started ganging up on me. One I could handle, but not more than that."

Silas met Tyrone's stare. He had no doubt they were both thinking of their hellcat of a mother. She didn't need a lot of extra anything, she was already tough.

He turned back to Arianna and wondered if that was her birth name. They'd need her original name to check out her story, but he'd let Theron deal with that later.

"How long are your pregnancies?"

She squinted and looked at the other two. "Six – seven months, wouldn't you say?"

Leann nodded. "About that for twins anyway. Shorter for quads."

"Have you ever given birth to human babies?" Silas asked the woman on the couch.

"No. I don't think I've ever met a human," Leara said.

"Me neither," Leann said, nodding.

Silas tented his fingertips beneath his lips. "I sensed three human heartbeats before entering this compound. Leara, you say you've never met a human, yet you appear to be human." He ignored her scared wide eyes as she looked at him and then at Arianna.

"You too, Leann." His gaze swung to Arianna. "Who were their fathers?" His eyes blazed, daring her to lie.

Arianna shrugged unconcerned. "I don't remember, maybe Pedro or Miguel the beta. When I first arrived, he refused to allow anyone else near me. Ask Anna, the housekeeper, she knows everything that happens here."

He released a long sigh as he contacted Theron through their link. *"Send Anna the housekeeper to the office."*

Silas gritted his teeth in aggravation. "This is bullshit. Who the hell is messing with the natural order of things? A rape that took place over one hundred years ago has snowballed with serious repercussions. And you may not have been the first or the last." He raked his hand through his hair.

A knock sounded.

Tyrone opened the door. The tiny woman who'd greeted them earlier stepped in, her eyes round with fear. She frowned when she noticed the women sitting quietly. "Yes?"

Silas pointed to another chair. "Please, have a seat. I have questions to ask you. I'd appreciate any help you can give me."

She swallowed hard and took a seat. "I'll do my best."

Silas noticed her lack of Spanish accent and wondered about her origins. But he had more pressing matters. "Do you know who sired

Leann and Leara?"

"Yes, Sir. Pedro."

"What happened to the other female pups she birthed?" He tipped his head in Arianna's direction. It was a waste of time to discuss biology with the women. Somehow, the women showed up as humans even though they were half-wolf. It didn't make sense. None of this made sense.

"Yes, Sir. Pedro sold them."

A flare of anger flashed through Silas and the women screamed. He calmed himself. *"Everything okay?"* Theron asked through their link.

"Yes. Is Pedro dead?"

"Yeah. Why?"

"I'd like to kill him." Silas broke the link. The small woman was shaking in the chair. He hadn't meant to frighten her.

"Anna? That's your name, right?"

Her head jerked up and then down.

"I apologize for frightening you. I am angry that Pedro sold the woman, that's all. Can you tell me what happened?"

After taking three deep breaths, the woman spoke. "Pedro told me to get rooms ready, we were having guests. Important guests. When the men came, they talked for a while. Had a meal and then went to the two rooms I'd prepared for them. He sent Stephanie and Maria to spend the night with them. The guests stayed a week. When they left, they took the girls with them because they were breeding."

"Breeding?" Silas wanted to be sure. "Pregnant with babies inside their stomachs?"

Anna shrugged. "I don't know what to call them, but they were breeding when they left."

"Leann and Leara are unmated wolves with the ability to give birth, another anomaly. We need to know how they felt when this happened, where were they when they realized they had the potential to give birth. Were they raised by the wolves? Or are the female hybrids given special treatment? Tyrese interview Leann. I want you

to get her life story. They are half wolves, do they shift? Or is that ability lost? Get personal, we need to know everything. Tyrone, you're on Leara. I'll finish with Arianna and we'll compare notes later," he told them. They needed to make up time.

Silas ushered Anna closer so the three of them could talk. In his experience, servants saw and knew more than people gave them credit.

The next hour and a half, the light buzz of conversation filled the room. Silas discovered Pedro dabbled in criminal activity, something he told Theron immediately. He learned once the women birthed the pups the wolves raised them. The human breeders did not interact with the pups. He thought that was strange, but listened rather than question their motives.

All in all, Silas discovered the breeders healed fast and could accommodate the roughest wolf without breaking. There was something about giving birth that kept them young and viable with the ability to keep reproducing. If it didn't violate so many laws of nature, he'd clap his hands in awe. But he'd lived long enough to know rules might be stretched without much penalty, but when broken, there was always hell to pay.

Standing, Silas brought all conversations to a halt. "Thank you for your help. We have just learned of your existence and required more information. Pedro is dead. Philippe won the leadership challenge and will be the new pack leader under Alpha Theron. He will meet with all of you later. You are free to live wherever you please. You can stay with this Pack or I will send you anywhere you want." He looked at each of them. "The choice is yours."

"I will go with you," Arianna spoke into the silence. "I will help you build your pack."

Leann and Leara bit their lips and turned away, but Silas saw the laughter in their eyes.

Anna rolled her eyes. The servant had been helpful filling in the blanks and he knew she saw more than many realized. He'd make sure Theron placed her in a position among the wolves.

"I think you misunderstood. I have no Pack," Silas said as he straightened his shirt and brushed off his pants.

"You have many sons?" Arianna asked, frowning.

"I guess you can say that. But I have no Pack, so choose somewhere else or stay here. It's up to you." He turned to leave when she spoke.

"I would serve you well, Silas Knight. Take me with you."

He ignored her and walked out of the room.

Chapter 12

SILAS, TYRONE, AND TYRESE drove in silence as they returned to the Maryland compound. The trip to Mexico answered questions but raised a lot more. None of this made any sense. How could a man rape a woman and change her biology? Was there a purpose or just random bad luck? A disease, perhaps?

"I'm holding an Alpha conference in three hours in the lodge; I want the two of you there."

"Yes, Sir," Tyrone said, watching the road while Tyrese drove.

Silas smothered a grin. It was amazing what proper training would do for a man. The twins' physical and mental abilities impressed him. He'd decided to place them on his personal security detail after he'd seen them fight Jayden. His Alpha admitted how good the boys fought. Besides, since no one knew much about how hybrids functioned, it was better to keep them close.

"Drop me off at the main building."

"Yes, Sir."

Jayden had taken offense at what he deemed a too casual demeanor toward Silas and drilled the twins in proper protocol. As former soldiers, it didn't take long for them to have a solid grasp of pack politics and hierarchy.

Once they reached pack grounds, the scenery changed. Jayden honored the earth and went to great lengths to keep things natural. Silas relaxed as the fragrance of the flowers and greenery teased his nostrils. The buzz of insects and laughter of pups in the distance blew past his ears. His wolf took noticed and whined. He'd love to run, but there were so many things he needed to accomplish before his meeting.

Silas pinched the bridge of his nose as his thoughts drifted to Jasmine. He wondered if she was okay. Had she thought about him? Was she breeding? A frisson of distaste hit the back of his throat. A gift of half-breed pups would be a slap in the face.

He was the Patron of the wolf. Not of the half-wolf. But his wolf had refused to be denied, and he'd complied by releasing his seed. Nothing to do now but wait and see. Over the years he'd wondered why his seed had never taken root. He'd asked the Goddess once, She'd cautioned him to be patient. Had he waited hundreds of years for half-wolf pups? He loathed the idea.

The car pulled up to Jayden's home. Tyrone got out and opened Silas's door while Tyrese grabbed his luggage from the trunk. After walking Silas inside, Tyrese released the luggage.

"We'll be back at eighteen hundred hours, Sir."

Silas nodded and headed toward the stairs. One of the Pack's omegas took the luggage to his room while Jayden met him in the hall.

"Good trip?" Jayden asked as they walked toward the office.

Silas stripped off his lightweight jacket and hung it on the back of one of the office chairs. "Yeah. Too much information. This thing has been going on much longer than we thought. The human breeder I met was over a hundred years old."

Jayden's eyes widened. "What?"

Silas slapped him on the back. "Yeah. Alpha conference in two and a half hours. Set up the room, bring my laptop, I've got a lot to pull together in a short amount of time."

"How...?"

"Hold your questions for the meeting. I'd prefer to give the news once." Silas strode to the desk, please to see his laptop already there, and got busy.

* * *

Tyrese parked the car in the condo's parking area. When he opened his door, Tyrone halted him.

"We lucked out, you know." Tyrone closed his eyes and then looked at him. "I mean with Mom. I looked at those wolves and realized the only identity they had was in those walls. They had no clue about family. Nobody loves them." He shook his head.

Tyrese understood. "That's a big problem with this breeder deal. A wolf's bitch cares and nurtures her pups. It makes us who we are, instills a sense of pride, of belonging." He shook his head. "They and a lot of the wolves Arianna birthed don't have that. Chances are they're unstable, and don't understand what the den and Pack means."

"There's bullshit brewing out there, that's for damn sure. I mean those women were human, or at least a big part of them is human." Tyrone said. "But Silas didn't sense a wolf inside them." He scratched his head. "That's weird. I thought the wolf gene was dominant."

Tyrese shrugged. Leann had been shy at first, but the longer they talked she answered all of his questions. A wolf attracted her early on and they'd had sex. When she became pregnant, Pedro had her moved to the Alpha house. Her first set of twins were girls. One was sick, and she'd heard Pedro had killed the pup. She had no idea what happened to the other. From that time, she'd stayed in the Alpha house and laid with the men her Alpha brought to her. After her first set of female pups, the rest had been all-male litters, but many had physical problems like shorter legs, one blind eye, heart, and breathing problems. Pedro always terminated the lives of those pups.

"They're not wolves. Just like Mom's, not a wolf. She's... different."

Tyrone nodded, although he still wore a deep frown. "Were you surprised Leann and Leara decided to stay with the pack and move to Texas with Theron instead of trying to start their lives over somewhere new?"

"Not really," Tyrese said. "That pack is all they know, and once Theron discovered Pedro dealt with the drug cartel, he had to move the pack to Texas for protection."

Tyrone nodded and looked at him. "What do you think about all of this? About Mom? Silas? Mom having pups. Is she like Arianna?" He shook his head. "Not her personality, Mom is all about fam. But the healing? And being able to run or fight?"

Tyrese chuckled. "I wouldn't put it past her. She's mean when she's mad. Always has been. But the thing is," he lowered his voice. "If Mom's a breeder, so is Aunty. Plus they don't grow old like normal."

"Damn, I hadn't thought about Aunty. You think Mandy's one of those breeders and they got together? That'd be cool," Tyrone said, smiling.

"Yeah, but not likely," Tyrese said. "But the thing that'd bothered me for a long time was her leaving... you know? Mom dying. While we'd be left here a long while. It used to bother me big time. Now..."

"Now we don't have to worry about that."

"But they live longer when they have pups, Mom just has us," Tyrese said in a pensive tone.

"Um... if she's not pregnant after that damn marathon with Silas, then it's not going to happen. If I never hear my momma scream like that again it'd suit me fine," Tyrone said, shaking.

Tyrese laughed, although he hadn't been laughing that day when his mom and Silas had sex. He'd covered his head with pillows, turned up the TV and music to block her moans and demands. It still embarrassed him to remember how she'd demanded Silas.... He couldn't go back there either.

After Silas had left, she'd remained in her room the rest of the day. He'd swear she tiptoed out around four in the morning, grabbed a bite of food, and ran back to her room. It took another day for her to face them, and then she'd refused to look at them. Callum was the only person she seemed comfortable around these days.

The Mexico trip had come at the best time.

"I'm with you on that." Tyrese inhaled. "But we are lucky to have her."

On that note, they exited the car and headed upstairs. The moment they turned the corner to the condo, their stomachs growled and huge smiles split their faces.

"Mama's cooking."

Tyrese inhaled. "I smell baked chicken and yellow rice."

"Candied yams?" He looked at his brother in shock and excitement.

"Greens and cornbread," Tyrone said after taking another sniff. "There's cake. She baked a cake, man," he said, bouncing as he opened the door.

"And that's how you do it. Taste this," Jasmine said to Callum, placing a spoon near his mouth. She looked up as the door opened.

"Hi, when'd you boys get back?" she asked as she put down the spoon and walked out of the kitchen. Arms outstretched, she hugged Tyrone and then Tyrese.

Tyrese looked at the plates with half-eaten food and prayed there was more.

"Why didn't you call and let me know you were on your way home?" she asked over her shoulder as she returned to the kitchen.

"We were in a hurry and didn't think about it until a few minutes ago. What're you doing?" He didn't bother to recognize the little imp who was always underfoot these days.

"I'm teaching Callum how to cook and he's doing a great job. We baked today." She looked around the kitchen and then back up at them. Her dark brown eyes sparkled. "Hungry?"

"Yes, starving. Something smells good," Tyrone said, moving into the kitchen. Tyrese watched Callum, he didn't trust the smirk on the teenager's face.

"I'll fix you guys a couple of sandwiches then, just give me a few minutes," she said, placing her hands on her hips. "We didn't cook enough for the two of you since I didn't expect you."

Callum turned away laughing.

His mom's face glowed with happiness. She'd done something different with her hair, the curls fell around her shoulders.

Tyrese strode forward, pulled her in his arms. "You're right, mom. I should've called. I'll fix a sandwich or something." He placed a kiss on her cheek. "You are one beautiful lady and I'm glad you're my mom."

Her eyes widened as they filled. "Aww, thanks, honey." She kissed him on the cheek and then leaned back, frowning. "Everything alright? The trip went okay?" She looked at Tyrone who'd moved close.

The front door closed. Callum had left, smart kid.

"We met three human women who've birthed wolves. They were pregnant," Tyrese said.

"Let me hug her for a minute. I missed you, too." Tyrone edged in and kissed her cheeks. "You are beautiful and I'm just... so happy to have you in my life." He kissed her again.

She held him tight and then took his hands. "Okay, sit at the table and tell me what happened while I fix you something to eat."

Tyrone looked at her plate. "You don't have any more left?"

"I do, but not enough. I'll fix more, it won't take long. Now sit down and tell me about these women that got you running home to your mama."

Tyrese groaned as he took a seat.

Tyrone laughed, picked up an apple, threw it to his brother, and then got another one. He bit into it and chuckled. "That's a good one, ma, and true on so many levels. There was this woman, her name's Arianna."

Over the next hour, they filled her in on the unclassified part of their trip. They ate and answered her questions until she'd run out of steam.

"Wow. This is hard to believe. What if she's like my great-great-grandmother or something?"

"I doubt that?" Tyrone said. Tyrese sent him a pitying look for speaking without thinking.

She arched her brow. "Why?"

"You don't look like her." He frowned at Tyrese.

"You don't look like me and I'm your mother. I guarantee you that. I've got the blood tests to prove it. You wanna explain again why this woman can't be related to me?" Her voice hardened.

There was one thing Jasmine Bennett hated. Bigotry. She'd drilled it into them when they were small. If something had a sniff of it in any form, she'd get riled. As kids, they knew better than to ever tease a child or adult who looked different or had special challenges. She had zero tolerance for slurs or slights. In high school, he and Tyrone had been popular because they accepted everybody as friends. Not best friends, but friends.

Tyrone sighed. "I'm sorry. I guess I don't want her to be related, so that's why I said that. She's creepy, Mom."

"She's old and grew up in a different era. You'd be creepy too." She smacked his hand as she stood. "I thought you guys had a meeting?"

Tyrese jumped up, looked at his watch, and cursed. He pecked her on the cheek and headed for the door, Tyrone behind him. They had ten minutes.

Chapter 13

JASMINE WATCHED THE DOOR close and walked over to lock it. Disturbed, she went over everything the boys had told her. Someone raped the woman, and she gave birth to twins. After tidying the kitchen, she picked up her phone and placed a call.

On the second ring, a voice answered. "Mom?"

"Jasmine, honey, it's good to hear your voice."

She bit down on her lip before responding. "How are you and Mark?"

"We're good. The boys?" her mom asked with hesitation.

"Rone's in therapy from his accident and Rese is here helping him. They're both doing okay." She paused, choked back the dread threatening to overwhelm her, and pushed forward. "Mom didn't you tell me I had a twin, but she died at birth?"

There was a discernible pause. "Yeah, little Janay. She had heart problems and didn't make it, why?"

"I was just curious. The boys were telling me about this woman who was raped, she'd had twin girls but something happened to one of the girls. Somebody took her they said."

Her mom gasped. "Raped?"

"Yeah, he raped her and passed on a virus, I'm not sure about everything, but I was curious." She said just enough to get her mom thinking. If she was lucky the woman would open up and tell her more about their past. To date, her mom never discussed anything before meeting her husband. The fact he wasn't their biological dad slipped out one day in the heat of an argument. Her mom denied ever saying it, but she and Renee had never forgotten.

"Curious about what?" her mom snapped.

"Everything and nothing. How long you guys going to be in Miami?" She changed the subject knowing her mom wouldn't let it rest.

"Another week. What kind of virus?"

"Huh?"

"You said something about a virus during the rape. What kind? Did the boys say?"

"Something about it slowing down aging, helped the person heal fast, gave 'em lots of energy, oh yeah and it makes you real fertile. Crazy huh?"

For a moment her mom didn't speak. "No, not really. Stranger things have happened."

Jasmine closed her eyes as she squeezed the phone tight. "Yeah? Like what?" She got out through a tight throat.

"Hold on a minute, let me close the door."

* * *

The house was dark. There was a light tap on the front door. Jasmine heard it, but after the bombshell her mom dropped on her a while ago, she didn't want to see or talk to anyone. Not even her sons.

The knock came again, harder this time.

Jasmine rolled over, covering her head with the pillow, expecting to hear feet leaving, not walking inside her home.

She shot up straight. Her heart slammed in her chest as she grabbed her throat.

"Jasmine."

Her lids lowered in relief and then snapped open in anger. "Silas. I don't feel like company. That's why I didn't answer the door."

He walked into her bedroom, smelling like outdoors and looking, outright male. Her nipples tingled in recognition as he leaned against the opening.

"The twins went out with the Pack and I told them I'd check on you. They called, but no one answered." He stepped into the dim room.

Her heart raced as a sliver of light from outside hit the planes of his face. He looked big, menacing, and well, damn good. "I'm fine, thanks," she said in a dismissive tone, hoping he'd take the hint and leave.

He sat on the edge of the bed and leaned forward, elbows on his knees. "What happened?"

"Huh?"

"You're upset. What happened?" His demanding tone irritated her.

"Nothing I want to discuss." She pulled her legs up out of the way.

"You prefer to be fucked?"

She shook her head at the change in topic. "No. I prefer to be alone."

"Talk or fuck, it's up to you."

He stood, toed off his shoes, and unbuttoned his shirt. A deep throb started low in her belly. Tingles of anticipation ran amok inside her. She closed her eyes to gain control and swallowed hard.

"Stop Silas." She ground her teeth in frustration. "I found out something a little while ago from my mom and I'm trying to process it. I don't want to have sex and I don't want to talk."

"We'll ignore the lie about sex, but if this has something to do with your ability to breed wolves, I'd like to know what you discovered." He returned to the side of the bed in just his pants.

She frowned and sat back against the headboard. "Does it matter that I don't want to be bothered with you?"

"Sometimes, just not this time."

She crossed her arms over her chest. "You know… I don't have to tell you anything. I'm not a wolf or a member of your pack or your organization or whatever you call it. I have a life of my own and I'd like to get back to living it again. When will I be able to leave? Or am I a prisoner here?"

They stared at one another for a moment. "You're right. You're not a wolf, although I suspect you have a lot of our traits. You understand pack protocol, so I know you're just being ornery right now. Tyrese told me they shared what we found in Mexico, so you are aware other human females breed. And I'll release you after your next cycle."

Her head snapped back. "What? Why wait?"

His brow raised a notch. "Pups. We'll know by then if you're breeding or not."

Her stomach twisted, and she sank further down the bed. She was almost certain she was pregnant but didn't want to take a test and seal her fate. There were so many things she wanted to explore in her life before raising more kids.

"What happened, Jasmine?" He lay across the bed, trapping her legs. He leaned on his elbow and stared at her. His eyes, more blue than green, tempted her to give into him.

She looked up at the ceiling. It didn't offer a reprieve or make the news any better. "A man raped my mom," she whispered. Answering the question she'd put to Tyrone earlier. Arianna was not a relative.

He tensed but didn't move.

"I had a twin, but she died from a severe birth defect. Mom was still tore up about it as she told me. My twin's organs, they were all wrong, they didn't work or something." He rubbed her arm while she got her breathing under control.

"Renee's older and from the man I thought was my father. My twin and I were from the rape. Since then, my mom has had at least ten abortions. The last one a year ago. She refuses to have any more children after my twin's deformity." Tears filled her eyes. They hadn't asked for any of this. Now, she and her mother might outlive her sister. Her sixty-year-old mother still looked half her age and dated men much younger.

"I don't want this," she said, her voice cracking as she looked at him.

He scooted forward and held her beneath the shelter of his arm as tears filled her eyes. "I know, Jasmine. But in life we have to deal with the hand we're dealt. You're strong and there's a reason you carry this burden. We don't know why, but you have to trust that things will work out." He rubbed her back, soothing her.

"How old is your mom?"

"She just turned sixty last year, why?" She leaned into him, filling her nostrils with his woodsy scent.

"Arianna's rape happened when she was in her early twenties. So was your mom. So we know whoever is doing this has a thing for younger women, but not children, at least as far as we know he hasn't raped women under the age of twenty. Plus, he was still doing this thirty-five years ago. That's a serious block of time from Arianna to your mom."

She nodded as understanding dawned. "Did he rape a woman a year, every other year, or every decade? It's no telling how many women are infected." She looked up at him. "What does this mean? What are you going to do?"

Their eyes met. His had darkened to green. "Right now or later?" he asked in a slow sexy drawl that had her libido doing flips.

Her tongue swept across her dry lips. His eyes followed the movement. And then he crushed her to his side.

"Are you feeling better?" he growled.

"No, not really," she said to see what he'd do next.

He whistled a long sigh above her head. "What else troubles you?"

"I'm worried about my sons and what all this means. You call them half-breeds or hybrids. Just how different are they? And does their difference matter? Are they in danger or do you consider them a threat?"

She felt the groan through his chest as she settled back against the headboard.

"I'm not sure what this means. Someone has been upsetting the balance for years and we're just finding out. There's no telling how many hybrid wolves are out there or how many human breeders. Rone and Rese are exceptional wolves. They run as fast and are as strong as my trained Alphas."

"But the Mexican hybrids weren't. Not even close. Even those who had training. So I can't tell you what matters or not yet, because I don't know. More research has to be done. Is it their diet that made them different? Or their childhood? Or maybe how they were taught?" He shook his head.

"There are so many unanswered questions that I can't say right now. But I can tell you this, right now I don't see your sons as a threat. And I don't think they are in any added danger. We're a social community. They're learning what it means to have a Pack behind them and that's a good thing." He stroked her shoulder.

She looked up at him, curious at the wistful tone in his voice. His hand reached beneath the sheet, touching her thigh and setting off sparks of banked longing.

"We need interaction with others. A simple touch." His fingertips trailed along her thigh. Goosebumps exploded over her skin.

"That is the dilemma of the lone wolf. He too finds himself in need at times. Times when it's damn inconvenient."

"In need?" Her brow arched as the pads of his fingers tapped across her panty-clad mound. "Am I throwing off the mating scent again?"

He stared down at her, capturing her gaze. There was something in his eyes. Something indefinable. He blinked, and it disappeared.

"No. There's no mating scent, not this time." He paused and looked at her. "Jasmine, there's something you need to understand. I'm an older wolf who leads a nation of wolves, that's my first priority. I've seen a lot of things and done more than I have time to discuss. I don't have a mate, although I do have a servant who sees to my needs when I am in residence."

She frowned. "Huh?"

He shook his head. "That's not important unless you're breeding. Jacques will be the one to see to your care and then help with their upbringing."

"What?" She tried to lean forward, but he held her tight.

"Stop getting so riled. You're a little hellcat at times."

She cocked her brow at him. "You've lost your mind if you think anyone other than me is going to raise my kids. Don't even think I'd give them up to you or anybody else."

He shook her a few times. "I didn't say... didn't mean you'd be giving up the pups. I have servants in my home and one in particular whom I'd trust to deal with my litter. He has been with me for a hundred years and runs my home."

"So why'd you mention him? Are you lovers or something?" She eyed him.

He grinned, but it was far from innocent. She shivered as his eyes slid over her from top to bottom.

"I say he's my servant, you ask if he's my lover? That's a jump even for you. Where is your mind?" He flicked the hard bud of her nipple.

Her hand flew up and covered her chest. "Stop that. Go back to being an old fart, I mean wolf. I mean an old wolf." She smiled at his glower.

His face changed as he stared at her. A green starburst filled his eyes. Her breath caught, but she didn't look away. Heat filled her belly. Small tingles pricked her skin, not pleasurable, but not painful either.

Her breath hitched as she watched his eyes change to a mixture of green and blue. The seconds ticked without either of them speaking. Her fingertips itched to touch his face, not in a sexual way. Even in the quiet of the room, she sensed his leashed power, the warmth of it pulsed through the room. The idea of a quiet storm summed up the intensity of his eyes. Dark strands of her hair lifted beneath the wind of his glowing eyes.

"Why are you doing this?" she whispered, her eyelids heavy.

"I needed to see you. Your aura... it's unique." He placed a kiss on her forehead and inhaled her scent. Holding her tight against his chest, she wanted to ask him what he'd wanted to tell her, but the heaviness in her limbs lulled her asleep.

Chapter 14

SILAS LISTENED TO HER slow breaths as she drifted to sleep. It wasn't often the Goddess spoke to him in such a strong manner. With care, he released Jasmine, made sure she lay comfortable and stepped away from the bed. After one last look, he walked out of her bedroom and closed the door. He made it to the sofa, closed his eyes, and released himself.

His eyes opened, and he saw his face reflected in a pool of water. The white garments he wore surprised him, but he remained silent, on his knees in a position of deference. Head bowed, he waited.

"Patron of the wolves, rise." The words flowed through him, offering aid as he stood. The water shimmered as a silhouette of a wolf formed, then changed to the human form, and then changed to another beast's form. Puzzled, Silas watched and waited for an explanation.

"The one definite thing is change. It's coming with a time of testing. Your obedience and service to me have not gone unnoticed. You will be rewarded, although it may not seem so at the time. Be vigilant, you'll need your eyes to see. Be faithful, you'll need your ears to ferret out the truth. Be merciful, your nose will lead you to understand. Be courageous, your heart will suffer but will guide you to the truth. Taste the truth and embrace it, reject the lies and you will ride the wave of change. Your wolves need your direction now more than ever."

"Goddess, I don't understand what you mean by change."

Her voice blew in the wind, filling him. "You will. It comes now on the horse of fire."

He opened his mouth, a whirlwind of power swept around him. His arms and legs twitched as electrical currents flowed through him. It lasted seconds, although it felt like an hour or so. When it stopped, his head flopped back on the sofa.

Sofa?

He peeked. A kitchen was to the right. He sat in the middle of the living room floor, leaning against the furniture. Panting, he felt as though he'd just run a marathon. A pulse throbbed in his forehead as the words the Goddess spoke spun in vicious circles like victims of the whirlwind. Her words were like a puzzle, always had been. He wondered for the hundredth time, why She didn't just come right out and say what she meant?

Sighing, he pulled up to a sitting position and rested his forehead against his knee. It'd been a long day. The Mexican discovery. The deal with half-breed women retaining their humanity. The old breeder. He still couldn't believe she was that old, but her story had checked out. Arianna Hershman had vanished. Her teenage daughter had returned home but ran away again. They hadn't been able to find the other daughter. She'd disappeared once she left for the Peace Corps. They were tracking down the sons to see if anyone had kept in contact over the years. It was a long shot, but it was a thread. And right now they needed to pull every thread no matter how thin.

There was a stirring in his mind telling him the person was a great distance from him. A second later he straightened as he recognized it was Theron.

"Theron?"

"Patron, rogues attacked us after we cleared customs." Silas could hear his Alpha's pain through the link. He cursed the distance.

"Tell me what happened." He picked up his cell and called the pilot. "Prepare the plane. We need to return to Texas, within the hour." He clicked off as he listened to Theron talk of the ambush. Twenty of the Mexican wolves suffered injuries. Three were dead.

"I'm on my way. Where are you now?"

"My pack just arrived and routed the bastards. I'd called to have them meet us at the border. That's why the death count is so low." He paused. "These wolves... they were fast and vicious. Their level of coordination surprised me. I haven't seen anything like it outside of training with you."

Silas tensed. *"I'm on my way. I'll meet you at the Alpha house. See to your pack."* Silas clicked off and studied the blank wall. In silence, he went over the words of the Goddess. "Horse of fire?" he muttered, wondering what it all meant. He shook it off and contacted Jayden.

"Someone ambushed Theron, I'm returning to Texas. Have my luggage sent to the plane while I contact my security."

"Are you taking the twins?"

Silas thought for a moment what Theron had said about the wolves who attacked them. If it was as he suspected, he'd need the twins to give him insight. *"Yes. Watch over Jasmine, she's breeding. No harm should come to her or her litter."*

"I understand. Congratulations."

Silas grunted. *"Hold off on that. I'm not excited over the prospect of hybrids yet."* He pulled open the door, locked it behind him, and headed for the stairs.

"I count it an honor to watch over your pups and the bitch who breeds them," Jayden said in a humble tone.

The comment pulled Silas out of his funk. "Thank you, Jayden. I cannot think of anyone else I'd trust to watch over their care." He walked out into the night and headed toward the garage. "I must assemble my team. When we arrive, I will contact you."

Within the hour, a somber Tyrone and concerned Tyrese were on the plane, along with Brad and Hank, two of his primary security team. Silas filled the men in with the little information he knew.

"That's unbelievable." Brad tugged on his goatee. "When was the last time anyone attacked an Alpha?"

Silas gazed out the window, muddling through the Goddess's words. "Over a hundred years," he answered.

"Why now?" Tyrone asked, puzzled.

"Perhaps no one taught them not to attack an Alpha. Maybe they don't understand the hierarchy," Tyrese mumbled, brows furrowed.

"Could be," Brad said, looking at Tyrese. "Who taught you?"

Tyrese shrugged. "Alpha Jayden."

"Yeah, being military brats helped. We knew there was always a chain of command. Dad, then Mom..." Tyrone said.

Brad nodded. "What do you think would'a happened if you didn't have that?"

Tyrese shrugged, looking at Brad. "What happens to any wolf who's alone? I'd make up my own rules. And if I met others like me, I'd teach them my rules, not somebody else's."

Tyrone looked between Brad and Tyrese. "You think that's what happened?"

Brad shrugged. "It wasn't a lone wolf who attacked over forty wolves. Those numbers alone would make most wolves back off and rethink the situation. Whoever did this recognized the caliber of the wolves and had a serious dose of confidence."

"Alpha?" Hank asked.

Brad shrugged. "I wasn't there, but if not a trained Alpha, then someone with the skills. It might help to look through the list of applicants to train with the Patron for Alpha status. Maybe someone in this area is tired of waiting."

Silas listened and thought the idea had merit. "I'll have Jacques begin the search. We'll give him more info after we talk with Theron."

It was after three in the morning when the plane set down in Texas. Tired and operating on fumes, Silas rode in the car to Theron's pack lands. He was the only one awake other than the driver. When he stepped in the car, he'd contacted Theron through their link when he scented the driver and knew he wasn't from the alpha's Pack.

They turned off onto a dirt road and came to a stop. Silas woke his team with a mental slap, cautioning them to silence as they waited to see how things played out. A group of five wolves stood in front of the vehicle.

Tyrese opened the door and stepped out, Tyrone behind him. The wolves snarled at the twins. Tyrone closed the door as Brad snapped the neck of the driver.

"How many?" Tyrese asked Silas.

"Those in the road, three more in the bushes." He paused. "One is human."

"Damn," Tyrone groaned. "Not this shit again."

The wolves snapped and lurched forward as though held by an unseen leash. Silas felt the twins hum with energy. They wanted to fight. Five against two in their minds was no big deal despite what Theron had experienced.

"These wolves are trained to fight like one," Silas cautioned. "Hank is coming to even the odds."

Hank stepped out from the back seat, the wolves had snarled before, now they went ballistic.

Silas considered slaying the wolves outright, but wanted to see their capabilities. Plus he was curious about the others in the bushes. One thing for certain, he would not allow them to escape.

Tyrone and Tyrese leapt and landed in front of Hank.

The older wolf growled his displeasure, shifted, and stood next to the twins. His wolf snarled as eager as the other wolves. Silas stepped out of the car and called the wolves hiding in the bush into the light. Struggling against his compulsion, they yipped and snarled as they came into the clearing.

Seeing the wolves struggling, the other wolves lunged toward the twins and Hank. Silas watched the battle while holding the two wolves hostage. Theron had been right; these wolves were fast but not as fast as the twins.

Silas watched as Tyrone and Tyrese shifted, raced around the wolves in a blazing circle, snipping and taking swipes with their claws.

One wolf leapt forward outside the circle and Hank was on it at once.

The remaining wolves tried to catch one of the twins, but their speed was unbelievable. Tyrone stepped in and pushed one of the snarling wolves toward Hank, who bit its leg and then snapped its neck. Tyrese cut through the remaining three wolves and pushed another wolf aside. The wolf couldn't stand before Hank was on top of it.

"Stop!" A woman's voice called out as she strode through the clearing crying with wild eyes. Her hair tumbled in disarray around her shoulders and down her back. With jerky movements, she turned toward the two wolves Silas held.

"Stop them," she commanded. One wolf howled, while the other snapped at the woman. The human jumped back, looked between the two wolves, and the fight with a gleam of horror and fascination. She fell to her knees with a loud wail as the fight drew to conclusion.

Tyrese and Tyrone continued, and Silas had no intention of stopping the massacre.

Once the last of the five wolves were down, Tyrese, Tyrone, and Hank howled. Blood dripped from their sharp teeth as they turned their attention to the other two wolves and the human female who sat on the ground sobbing.

Silas stepped into the clearing. He heard Theron and his pack approaching and needed answers before he allowed the Alpha to extract his justice. He glanced at the twins. *"Good job,"* he told them and Hank through their links. The twins had worked as a synchronized unit that left their enemy confused. It was a brilliant strategy, he planned to talk with them about it later.

They howled and circled to come up behind him.

Silas looked at the two wolves. "Change."

Seconds later an older man and woman lay on the ground in front of him. They looked at the weeping female. The male made a move as though to comfort her.

Silas growled, and he froze. *"Brad, secure the female."* He sent the message and his bodyguard sauntered over to the woman, picked her up, and then dropped her. A long knife stuck out of Brad's chest. Silas's rage boiled over and he slapped the female with a whip of his power as he strode over to check on Brad.

Hank and the twins surrounded the couple on the ground as the male begged Silas to spare the female's life. The human female flipped on the ground as though currents of electricity ripped her apart. Silas hadn't gone easy on her.

No one attacked his guards. No one.

Kneeling beside Brad, he looked at the man. "See me."

Brad's eyes latched onto his.

With one move, he pulled out the knife. "Change." He sent a surge of compulsion in his words to aid the transformation so Brad could heal.

The rumble of vehicles signaled the arrival of Theron's pack. Seconds later they entered the clearing. Theron changed from a hulking wolf and strode to Silas. He bowed and looked at the dead wolves.

"You didn't save much for me." The man sounded disappointed.

"The twins got antsy and teamed up with Hank for baseball." He waved off Theron's frown. "Later, right now I'm waiting for Brad to stop lying around and stand." The wolf in question lifted his head, and then with slight hesitation stood and moved around slow.

Silas tipped his head in the female's direction. "She stabbed him."

Theron growled.

"Yeah. But I want to talk to all three of them before you mete out justice for your fallen."

Theron nodded although Silas could tell he wanted to rip the three apart. His pack stacked the dead wolves for transport back to their lands, where they'd dispose of them. He cuffed the two remaining wolves and stuffed them into vehicles.

Theron picked up the human female, daring her to do something. She closed her eyes as he took her to another vehicle.

Tyrone, Tyrese, and Hank changed at Silas' command. They watched Brad lope toward the car and change. In silence, Hank slid behind the wheel and pulled out behind the Alpha's car. The other cars pulled out behind them. The drive to the pack lands was in silence, although Silas knew questions swirled in the minds of the twins. He appreciated that they waited. One debriefing was more than enough.

Chapter 15

THE SPRAWLING TWO-STORY ALPHA house sat in the middle of ten thousand acres in the southwestern part of the state. Theron's Pack lands boasted of schools, a baseball and football field, a small hospital, a butcher, dry goods, a bar, and all types of small businesses. There were pastures with livestock, numerous barns, and large fields of crops. Pools and playgrounds dotted the landscape, as well as several homes in small communities.

It had been a while since Silas had visited. Theron and his mate Shelby, a licensed veterinarian, always impressed him with their forward thinking. At the mouth of their lands, a nice sized strip mall open to the public created jobs for Pack members. That's where Shelby opened her veterinarian practice, as well as a large grocery store, a drug store, and small department stores. A movie theater and karaoke bar sat on opposite ends of the mall. All employees lived on Pack lands. All deliveries for the Pack's stores and office shared a space. Theron's security teams enforced his strict rule of 'Pack only' on their lands.

Security took the wolf prisoners to the small jail while a doctor checked the female. She hadn't spoken since she'd screamed for them to stop killing the wolves. Shelby, Theron's mate, strolled into the room where Silas sat talking to Theron. The Alpha had a smile on his face before she spoke.

"Greetings, La Patron." The petite redhead with emerald green eyes that flashed fire when angry offered him a small bow with a large smile. He remembered when Theron courted the firebrand, her eyes flashed all the time. She hadn't wanted to give up her schooling and move to the country. A wolf's major strategy was to tire their opponents. Theron had been relentless in his pursuit and in the end, won his prize.

Silas took her tanned hand and placed a kiss on the back of it. "It's about time the light came into this dreary place." He smiled as her cheeks reddened. "You are still beautiful, Shelby. It's a pleasure to see you again. I wish the circumstances were better…"

She nodded and glanced at her mate. He reached for her. She stepped into his arms and he kissed her hard. Silas looked over their heads at the twins. They were in the middle of a discussion with Hank while Brad sat in a chair nearby, listening.

"The female is fine, a little shaken, but otherwise still angry and mouthing curses. We found this in the bushes. She recorded everything."

Silas looked at the cell phone. "Have you tracked her last call?"

"It went to an untraceable phone. But she'd taken pictures of the fight, no doubt sent them as well," Theron said looking at the device. Silas shrugged. "What about your wolves? The ones who suffered from the earlier attack?"

"They are healing." She chuckled. "Although Philippe has decided to pass on the Alpha position."

Silas looked between the two, wondering what he'd missed. "Why?"

Theron pulled his mate close and looked at him. "When we arrived, they couldn't believe Packs live like this. Within moments of eating a full meal in the hall, they all asked to join our pack and not return to Mexico. Philippe was the first to ask."

Silas nodded. "You've done well. There is a sense of growth and security here. I understand that most of your young return from college to either work here on the lands or in your shopping areas."

Theron nodded. "Yes, we're building a few office buildings here for new businesses. Shelby has approved the business plans for ten pack members. We'll build another structure near the strip mall for businesses that appeal to both sides of our nature."

"That's excellent," Silas said with pride. "I'd love to hear more about that tomorrow, now I'd like to talk to the wolves. And then the female."

Shelby nodded.

"Yes, Sir. This way, please. There's a holding section for the injured. The wolves are down this hall," Theron said, leading the way.

The chained wolves lowered their heads when Silas and Theron walked in alone. Silas watched the mated pair and wondered over their connection to the human female.

"Did your pack attack this pack earlier today as they crossed the border?" Silas asked.

The wolves frowned. "No. We are a small pack. To attack an Alpha is suicide."

"Yet you put one of your drivers in my car and had him take me to a side location. You didn't think that was suicide?"

The male blanched. "We didn't know who… she just said to take the car, to bring the car to the clearing."

"Who? Who told you to take the car?" They knew he was coming.

"Mar—"

The female stopped mid-sentence and looked at her mate. She snarled. "Even now you would protect her. After what she has done?"

"She didn't …"

"Of course she didn't, yet they are all dead. Dead because you chose to follow her instructions instead of listening to me. Me, your mate." She tried to swipe at him but her chains prevented the domestic brawl from escalating

Silas's brow rose. "This is the last time I will ask. Who told you to kidnap my car and how did you know I was coming?"

Theron tensed at the last question. It had been a long night and Silas forgave the Alpha for not realizing that important fact.

"It was Marguerite. The pack whore," she spat. "She's the human who's been breeding for my mate and the older wolves for the past fifty years. I've never been able to breed, and when one of the wolves brought her to the pack, they received her as a gift from the Goddess and gave her everything her heart desired. After a few deliveries, she started making suggestions on Pack activities. Instead of questioning her knowledge, the males jumped and did as she suggested."

"They were good ideas," her mate said, his face reddening as she spoke of him in a disrespectful tone. "You said nothing at the time."

Her head whipped around and she snarled. "I did. I questioned who she was and her ability to birth pups. That's not natural, damn you. Nor is it natural for you to mate with her, but you swore the Goddess favored you and allowed you to copulate with that bitch, and she bore you sons. She became your mate in all but name."

Silas heard the pain in the bitch's voice. The mating bond was sacrosanct. To hear that it had flaws, that it had been broken, sent a wave of trepidation through him. These humans threatened their existence.

"You violated your mating vows?" Theron asked, his voice deep, hard.

The male wolf jerked and stared a moment, before lowering his head. "I… At the time I didn't see it that way. My thoughts focused on having pups. Nothing more. I… I failed my mate and my pack."

"Where are the pups?" Silas couldn't believe that the five they'd disposed of earlier were all there were after fifty years.

"Half had problems, he killed them outright," the bitch said with sorrow. "Others died in fights, and others left to find their way in the world. The ones… the ones from tonight were the last of them."

"What about the older wolves? The ones who brought her to the pack? What happened to them?" Theron asked.

"Over time they died."

"You killed them, or had them killed," his mate snapped, disgust dripping from her tone. "You wanted no one else to fuck that bitch and got rid of them all."

"Yet you allowed your mate to live?" Silas asked, watching the male's reaction.

"I am a fool. I saw a gold ring and reached for it. I thought… I thought I received a second chance. I was wrong and my people paid for it." He turned to his mate. "You have hated me for a long time. I'm surprised you never killed her."

Her eyes blazed for a moment and then she looked away. "I loved the pups even though they weren't mine. I... I wanted the pups she provided." The shame in her confession tore through Silas.

"This is Alpha Theron of Texas. Earlier today a group like yours attacked his pack. The only reason I allowed the driver to take us to the clearing was to gain information. Once the wolves attacked, they were dead. Your fate is in Theron's hands."

He stepped out of the room to marshal his thoughts. The Mexican humans had no interest or involvement in Pack life. Yet this human ran the Pack through a weak Alpha. Like a wolf, the human must have sensed his weakness and used it to gain control over the small Pack.

But why? What'd she hope to gain? Tonight she'd lost it all. So far none of the dots connected. Theron stepped out of the holding cell and they proceeded to the small infirmary to talk with the human female. When they stepped inside, Silas froze at the sight of Leara and Leann talking to the bound female.

Theron's fury lit, and he leapt across the room, grabbed the women, and pushed them against the walls. They screamed. Their eyes widened in fright.

Shelby and her guards walked into the room. Tyrone, Tyrese, Hank, and Brad walked in and flanked him.

"Why are you in here?" Shelby growled at the women who shivered in fear.

Their mouths opened and closed, but no words formed. The stench of their fear filled the air. Shelby got up in their faces, snatched Leann by the hair to pull her toward her face.

"What the fuck are you doing in here? I'm not going to ask this nice again."

Silas withheld a chuckle at her version of nice.

"I thought... I heard someone calling me and... and I came to see what they wanted. I... I'm sorry. I didn't mean to do... I'm sorry." She slumped down crying.

Tears rolled down Leara's face as she watched her sister fall apart. "Honestly, we didn't realize this was wrong."

"I called them, they came." The human female said, watching Silas.

He'd sensed that's what happened but wanted it confirmed. There was something off with this human's scent. Something not quite right. Frowning, he tried to name the problem.

Shelby walked over to the female and growled. "You called them into my infirmary?" Theron stood behind his mate, blocking the human's view of Silas.

"Yes." There was no fear in the human's voice.

Theron grabbed Shelby and pulled her back to him. "If the Patron doesn't kill her, then I'll let you and the other women have her. She's been bad for the past few years," Theron's whisper was loud in the room.

The human laughed. It was warm and meant to seduce.

Although Silas's cock twitched, his wolf yawned as though bored. He smiled and released a pulse of energy into the room. It'd been a long day, and the sun was rising. He wanted this over so he could rest and decipher the Goddess' riddle.

The human screamed.

"Where are you from?" Silas asked in a bored tone. Theron continued to block him from the human

"Come here and ask –"

She screamed again.

Silas looked at Brad. "Take them out of here and don't let them out of your sight. They need a heart-to-heart discussion with their Alphas on pack protocol."

Leann and Leara's eyes widened as they looked at Theron and Shelby. Brad ushered them out of the room.

"Don't forget what I told you," the human screamed at their backs, spittle flying. Silas recognized the scent, the woman was mentally unstable. When she spoke, her words smelled bitter and stale. Shelby walked out behind the two women, taking her guard with her.

Theron braced his legs and crossed his arms in front of the human. "I don't think this one likes our hospitality. Permission to break her neck?"

"I fought the wolf bastards earlier for that honor," Hank said standing next to Theron. "If anyone should snap her neck, it should be me."

Silas smiled as the two bickered back and forth.

"How can you stand there and listen to … these animals talk of snapping a human's neck?" Silas looked up and realized the female was talking to the twins. Ah… now they were getting somewhere.

Tyrone shrugged.

"You're human. I feel that part of you." She frowned. "Why didn't you answer my call?"

"You called?" Tyrone asked. "I'm a wolf."

"No," the woman yelled, her face beet red. "You're human. A large part of you is human."

Tyrone shrugged and leaned against the wall watching her with a cheeky grin.

The female's mouth opened and then closed. "How'd they change you?" She eyed him with a smidgeon of suspicion.

"How'd they change you?" Tyrone asked.

"I was born with this curse."

"Me too."

The female gritted her teeth.

Silas listened with a smile. Tyrone was an excellent interrogator; he'd surprised them at how much information he was able to gather with little effort during their training drills.

"But you don't understand the importance of breaking free from their evil influence. You have to take control of your wolf and use your energies to change the way things are going. Each day we wake up with the knowledge that we're here for a reason. We have a higher purpose," the woman said with a fanatical edge.

"A higher purpose?" Tyrone said with the right amount of

eagerness.

"You are a superior wolf. Faster, stronger, and smarter than full bloods. Their time is coming to an end. You must train and prepare for change." She cackled, it was an eerie sound. "I'm weary of all this. It would be nice to see the end of the declaration, but like Moses, the promised land is denied to me. I made too many mistakes." She sighed. "Pride is a terrible thing. Mated pairs should never be disturbed." She released a breath.

Silas could hear the shock in the room.

"But tonight." She chuckled looking at the twins. "Tonight I saw the future. I hated to see my sons destroyed. They lacked the training that you and your brother had. But they still gave you a good fight? Right?"

Silas wondered what fight the woman had been watching. The twins had picked off those wolves with little interaction from the pack.

Tyrone pulled his earlobe. "Yeah... yeah, I gotta admit they had us on the run. But I'm not sure I understand what you mean by seeing the future. I mean, I'm younger than you by a few years, what'd you mean by that?"

"Youth. And I am more than a few years older than you, insolent pup." She smiled as she looked at him. "I'm going to die and I know it. Gerald was weak and allowed me to come between him, his mate, and his pack. Death was the outcome when I started that dance years ago." She shrugged. "But I grew impatient. I've been birthing pups for over a decade. Lost most of them, although a few survived. It seems the better technology became, the more pups survived. Anyway, I never agreed to do this forever. It shouldn't take this long."

"Huh?" Tyrone asked.

"Patience pup," she said with a frown.

"Shifters and humans. Separate, they're enemies. Put them together and what do you have?"

"Abominations," Theron growled.

The female twittered. "Look at these two, do they look like abominations to you?"

"They're wolves," Theron said.

"Not one hundred percent," the female snapped. "It's been hell finding a decent balance. Diet, exercise, upbringing, all of it plays a part." She sighed. "Patron. It's not that we don't respect your abilities, we do. But change is inevitable, we'd hoped to work with you, but we weren't ready and you're here." She shrugged. "And now we have a recording of what these wolves can do and you as well. We'll be better prepared now."

Silas suspected something like that, it was one of the reasons he held the two wolves immobile instead of killing them outright.

"But they were so excited watching the two of you fight," she said to the twins, who returned her stare. "Even now, they're researching your background so it can be duplicated. We figured something was missing and now we know."

"Yeah? What?" Tyrone asked his voice tight.

She cocked her head and looked at him. The light of insanity burned bright. "Pack. You need a tight unit of comrades, like a Pack."

Tyrone nodded. "You're right. Wolves can't survive without a Pack. The ones who try, go insane." He stared at her.

She smiled. "You are strong, I'm glad. Glad to see this hasn't all been in vain." She looked at Theron. "I'm tired. You can give me to the bitches now."

Chapter 16

SILAS LOOKED OUT OVER the compound. Tyrone and Tyrese had been quiet the day after Shelby and the other wolves attacked the human. The debriefing had included every Alpha who wore his crest. Some were skeptical over a possible plot to overthrow the current system, although they all admitted this enemy was harder to spot. Silas charged each of them to bind every Pack leader in their state to help ferret out potential upstarts.

The goddess' warning echoed the human's. Silas never believed in coincidences. It was imperative to get out ahead of the coming conflict. But was the conflict between half-breeds and full-bloods? Or something else? His first litter of pups would be breeds. He shook his head over the untenable position.

"Sir?" Tyrese called from the door.

"Enter." He'd been expecting them ever since Theron had called them abominations. He'd corrected all the Alphas against using the slur. Theron didn't see the twins in that light. Remarks spoken in the heat of the moment could still cause damage although the twins never flinched. But with his impending fatherhood, he wouldn't be as tolerant. As yet he'd not announcement of the future pups. He planned to wait for Jasmine to tell him and then he'd decide when to tell his Alphas. Most would be happy. Some would be disappointed. All would support him.

"The female spoke of researching our past and that's going to lead someone to our mother. We'd like to get her away from all of this.

Perhaps back home or to my aunt's for a break."

Silas shook his head. "She cannot leave my protection, she carries my pups."

"What?" Tyrese said. "She didn't mention it to us." He looked at his brother, who shook his head.

"She didn't mention it to me either so don't let on that you know," Silas said in a dry tone. "I searched and saw for myself. I told her that if she carried my pups, she'd have to live with me until she delivers them."

Tyrese laughed, but it lacked humor. "She'll never leave her kids."

"She told me that in colorful terms. Nevertheless, when we return to Maryland, I expect her to tell me she has my pups tucked away and to honor her end of the deal without dragging her feet."

"Her end of the deal?"

Silas remembered their discussion during their sexual escapades. "Ask her about it. But she'll be moving with me to my compound in West Virginia."

"Huh?" Tyrese looked sucker-punched. Tyrone's mouth gaped open. Both men looked lost and uncertain.

He looked at them. "You're welcome to come as well."

They brightened.

"Thanks. Wow, a brother or sister to watch over."

Tyrese smiled. "Yeah, now you have someone who might listen to all your bad advice." He smacked his brother on the back of his head.

"That's a bonus. But I call dibs on teaching the boys how to play football, you always ate my dust," Tyrone laughed, dodging his brother.

Silas listened as the two wolves bantered back and forth with a frown. Had he just lost control of the peace and quiet of his haven? How would Jasmine react when she realized he intended to move her as soon as possible? The human's mention of researching the twins had struck a nerve and he wanted her where he could protect her. Stifling a sigh, he looked at the twins and wondered, are they the future? If so how would they mesh with the present?

He stood, interrupting the twins. "I'm tired, and the plane is ready.

Time to get back to Maryland and then on to my home. I want your mom settled before we investigate your dad's pack."

At the mention of their father's former pack, the young wolves stilled. "You said we could travel with you when you met with them," Tyrese said, walking ahead of Silas while Tyrone brought up the rear.

Appearances be damned, he slowed and walked next to Tyrone. He didn't need a security detail but everyone had convinced themselves the wolves needed to see him separate and apart. He could speak through their link but didn't want to do that right now.

"I remember, and once we get Jasmine settled, we'll make plans," Silas said as they exited the building and headed for the cars that would take them to the airport.

Brad and Hank waited at the vehicle along with Shelby and Theron. Buck, their Beta, stood a short distance away.

Theron and Shelby bowed as Silas approached. "Thank you for honoring us with your presence, La Patron," Theron said as he shook Silas's hand.

Silas nodded, released his hand. He took Shelby's smaller one, kissed the back of it, and pulled her close. "Have I told you lately that you are one tough bitch?"

Shelby's face reddened. Her eyes lit with pleasure. "Yes, on more than one occasion." She laughed.

Silas nodded. "Good. I just wanted to be sure." He nodded to the beta and the wolves who'd come to see the Patron. The twins nodded to Theron as he shook their hands.

Hank held the back door open for Silas. As he stepped forward to enter the car, a cold wind blew across his face. The tiny hairs on the back of his neck rose in apprehension. He scented the air and scented nothing amiss, yet the sensation remained.

"Sir?" Tyrese asked in a quiet tone, while his eyes searched the area.

Silas stilled and looked back toward the second floor. Arianna stood in the window staring down at him, her eyes blazed for a moment and then returned to normal. In slow motion, she blew him a kiss.

Apprehension wrapped around him as he slid into the back of the car. "Goddess save me from fanatics," he muttered.

The End

A Note from Sydney:

Hello and thanks for taking the time to read my first book in the La Patron series. I love paranormal books and characters in general and shifter stories in particular. Throw in the romantic element, strong Alpha characters who bend beneath the power of love and I'm over the moon. Sighs...

I wanted an older heroine who'd had kids, experienced life in the "real" world first so that she could realistically handle an Alpha like Silas Knight. He's not easy but he loves fiercely and that's what Jasmine (and most of us) craves. Jasmine fit the casting call, with her set of twins, Tyrone and Tyrese. Their family dynamic blows me away every time the boys cater to their mom. Love it!

You're invited to journey with me through the six and counting books in this series. If you like fast-paced action, suspense, and great love connections like me, you won't be disappointed. Feel free to drop me a line, SydneyAddae@msn.com, or join La Patrons' Den, my Facebook group where discussions regarding Silas and the Wolf Nation abound.

For more information about Silas Knight and the Wolf Nation, I'd like to give you a **Free** *Companion PDF Booklet* with personal messages from Silas and Jasmine, as well as their family tree. To receive your Free Booklet and Free Book, go to my website www.SydneyAddae.com and join Knights Chronicles, my reading group, for fresh news on my Works in Progress.

La Patron, the Alpha's Alpha is my first paranormal series and I'd like to ask a favor. When you finish reading, please leave a review, whatever your opinion, I assure you I appreciate it.

Thanks again
Sydney

You've finished this story, get ready for the next! The following books are in the La Patron series, enjoy!

Birth Series
BirthRight
BirthControl
BirthMark
BirthStone
BirthDate
BirthSign

Sword Series
Sword of Inquest
Sword of Mercy
Sword of Justice

Holiday Series
La Patron's Christmas
La Patron's Christmas 2
La Patron's New Year
Christmas in the Nation

KnightForce Series
KnightForce 1
KnightForce Deuces
KnightForce Tres'
KnightForce Damian
KnightForce Ethan
Angus

LaPatron's Den Series
Jackie's Journey (La Patron's Den Book 1)
Alpha Awakening – Adam (La Patron's Den Book 2)
Renee's Renegade (La Patron's Den Book 3)
David's Dilemma (La Patron's Den Book 4)

Rise of the Wolf Nation Series
Knight Rescue - Rise of Wolf Nation 1
Knight Defense (Rise of Wolf Nation 2)

BlackWolf Series
BlackWolf Legacy
BlackWolf Preserved
BlackWolf Redemption

The Leviticus Club (The Olympus Project Book 1)

Altered Destiny
Family Ties

Booksets:
La Patron Series Books 1-3
La Patron Series Books 4-6
Sword Series
KnightForce Series Books 1-3
KnightForce Series Books 4-6
A Walk in the Nation (Three Stories to Tease Your Imagination

Other Books by Sydney Addae:
Last in Line (Vampires)
Bear with Me (Bear Shifter)
Jewel's Bear (Bear Shifter)
Do Over: Shelly's Surrender
Do Over: Rashan's Recovery
Secret of the Red Stone

www.SydneyAddae.com

Made in the USA
Monee, IL
19 November 2021